AF335341

By Larbi Layachi (Driss ben Hamed Charhadi)

A Life Full of Holes (1964)

LARBI LAYACHI

YESTERDAY AND TODAY

Black Sparrow Press
Santa Barbara--1985

Author's Acknowledgement: When people are good, you never forget them. I wish to express my gratitude to Helen S. Gross, Kathy Kerr-Schochet, Nancy McKee-Jolda, Katharine Harer, Duane Big Eagle, Mr. Z.B. Jackson, Debra Susan Gross, Ira Yeager, Jinny Sampson, Mr. and Mrs. Sampson, Mathew E. Kell, Kathleen Miller, Becky Reilly, Sallie F. Bell, Mr. and Mrs. Albert E. Schlesinger, Peter Pursley, Jetsin Eddy, Erle Rosolind, Dr. William F. Owen, Jr., Mr. and Mrs. Charles Lowe, Gary Starbuck, Mr. and Mrs. Starbuck, Tom Karnes, Patricia Allen, Charles and Etta Alston, Tsvi and Hyla, Paul Haverty, Sylvia Dea, Millicent G. Dillon, Peggy Mannion, Joe Mannion, Barbara D. Altafi, Larry Boxer, Dr. John Alden, Dr. George Maloof, Adib Nicola Dndum, Dr. Del Bosquvel, Dr. Julius Johnson, Mrs. Grace Covello, Dr. Rafaela Herrera, Michael Gross, Maral Good, Amy Neel, Mr. and Mrs. Samuel Neel, Jack Shatara, Nuha Shatara, Ann Paige Ewing, Maria Tersa Peri, Dr. John Simmons, Theresa V. Carey, Nan Bidinger, Danielle Epis, Mr. and Mrs. Curt Manning, Lynn Brown, Shellie Smith, Juliet Karnes, Laurent Broussal, Carlos Ramirez, Dr. W. Bradford DeLong, Masako Takahashi, Arlene Silverman.

LIBRARY OF CONGRESS CATALOGING IN PUBLICATION DATA

Charhadi, Driss ben Hamed, 1937-
Yesterday and today.

I. Title.
PS3553.H3215Y4 1985 813'.54 85-3912
ISBN 0-87685-632-6
ISBN 0-87685-631-8 (pbk.)

To Lady Jane with love.

I was hungry, and she fed me. I was cold, and she kept me warm.

She always spoke the truth.

To Lady Jane with love.

Contents

YESTERDAY
AND
TODAY

1 / The Baron

The summer of 1962 I was without work, as usual. One afternoon Lalla Ann Weston came looking for me and I wasn't home. She left a message with my wife that when I got home I was to see her. I wondered why Lalla Ann wanted to see me. The following day I went to see Lalla Ann at ten o'clock in the morning. I rang the bell and the maid opened the door for me. She said, "Come on in." I went straight in to the living room. Lalla Ann came out from another room and said, "Good morning, Larbi."

I said, "Good morning, Lalla Ann. My wife told me yesterday you were looking for me."

"Yes, I was looking for you. There is a man who is going to be living here in Tangier for the summer and he wants someone to work in his house. I thought you might be interested in working for this man."

"Of course. As you know, I'm always looking for a job."

"Why don't you come back tomorrow about ten or eleven o'clock in the morning and I'll take you to his apartment so you can talk to him about the job."

"Thank you, sweet lady, you've made my day." And I left.

The following day I went to see Lalla Ann at nine in the morning. She said, "Larbi, why did you come so early?"

I told her I was very excited about getting the job.

She said, "Sit down, won't you? Have some breakfast."

"No, thank you. I've had my breakfast."

"You must have something to drink—coffee or tea."

"I would like tea." She told the maid to make tea. I sat there drinking my tea. Lalla Ann was ready and she called a taxi. We left the apartment and took an elevator downstairs. We took a taxi down to the Avenida de España.

Lalla Ann showed the driver the house, and when we got there she paid the man and rang the bell. The man who opened the door was short and heavy and he had a very thick black moustache.

He said, "Good morning, Ann, come on in," and he hugged her and kissed her and said, "Sit down, sit down. Would you like to have some coffee?"

She said, "No."

He asked me if I wanted anything. I said no. Lalla Ann introduced me to him. She said to me, "This is the man who you are going to work for. His name is Mr. Mercer Saunders."

She said to Mercer, "This is Larbi. This is the man I told you about."

I shook his hand and he asked me if I wanted to work for him.

I said, "Ouakha."

He said, "Let me show you the apartment."

Lalla Ann stayed there talking to his secretary. He was a tall young man and very handsome. Mr. Mercer showed me all the rooms and said, "This is the apartment I want you to take care of."

I said, "Ouakha." I asked him how much he was going to pay me.

"I'll pay you 1,000 francs a day." Two dollars.

"Fine. I'll take the job. Can I start today?"

"No. You'd better start tomorrow. Let me give you a key. Tomorrow when you come you'll have your own key to get in with. Usually we leave by one o'clock. You can come in about that time and do your work and nobody will be here. You will have the apartment all to yourself."

I said, "Now I'm going to leave." I went to Lalla Ann who was sitting with the secretary and told her I got the job. I thanked her for recommending me.

I said, "I'm going to leave now. Are you going to stay?"

She said, "I'm going to stay here. I want to talk to Mercer."

I said, "Ouakha. Allah ihennik."

I left the apartment and went up to Zoco Chico to the Cafe de España where all the tourists go. I was looking for a friend of mine. I was going to work for him, helping him move. I promised him I would work for one week, and now that I had this job I didn't think I could do it.

I didn't find him. I went back home and told my wife about my new job. She asked me how long the job would last. I said, "Probably all summer."

The following day I got up early, I got dressed and washed and I left the house. I went down to the Zoco to a restaurant. I ordered a bowl of split pea soup and a half a loaf of bread. I had my breakfast.

The day was nice and warm. I decided to go to the

beach for a swim. I walked through town all the way to the Avenida de España. I crossed the railroad tracks and I got to the beach.

I took off my clothes and went for a swim. I stayed at the beach until twelve-thirty. Then I walked up to work.

I took the key and opened the door and I found Mr. Mercer and his secretary getting ready to leave. I said, "Buenas tardes," and they said, "Buenas tardes." I asked them if there were any special things they wanted me to do.

Mr. Mercer said, "No, you probably know what to do already. You do whatever you think is right."

"Fine."

"We're going to leave now. I believe you have everything you need."

"Yes."

They closed the door behind them. I went into the bedrooms first. I changed the sheets and I made the beds. I got the broom and I began to sweep until I had swept the whole apartment. Then I mopped the apartment. I cleaned the bathroom and it didn't take me very long. It took me about two hours to do the whole thing.

I said to myself, "I've made good time. One thousand francs is very good pay."

That was my job. That's what I was supposed to do. I took the trash basket downstairs and I dumped it in a barrel. I brought the basket back, I closed the door and I left.

I decided to go back to Zoco Chico to see if I could find the man I was supposed to help move. I found him in the Cafe de España. He asked me, "What happened? How come you didn't come yesterday?"

I said, "Yes, I was here yesterday about twelve o'clock. I couldn't find you here. I got a job and now I don't think I can help you, because this job is going to last longer than one week. If you want me, I could help you in the morning before one o'clock. I also could help you in the afternoon, after three o'clock."

"No. That wouldn't be good. I need someone all day long for a week. My mother is going to move in with me."

"Ouakha. I just came back to let you know what happened. I don't want to sacrifice a three month job to work one week for you."

He said, "I understand."

I said, "Allah ihennik." I went back home. My wife asked me how I liked the job. I said, "It is very good. You should get a job like that."

"Oh, no. I'm not going to work. That's why I married you, so you can work and support me."

"What's wrong with work? It would be nice if we could both work. Maybe if one of us loses a job, the other would have a job, so we wouldn't go hungry."

"No, no, no. I'm your wife, not your slave. I work in the house, not outside."

We kept arguing back and forth. I was getting very angry. I decided to leave the house for a while. I went down to the river. It was better than staying home arguing with my wife. I sat there by the river and I smoked a couple of cigarettes, listening to the water running down. I began to get sleepy.

When I got home, I found my wife's sister there. I said, "Ahilan," and I went to bed.

I slept until the morning. I got up, washed and left the house right away. I didn't even have breakfast. I went down to the port to see if there was any work for two or three hours. I walked around and I asked people, but there were no ships to unload. I decided to go to the cafe for a sfinj and a glass of tea.

It was about eleven-thirty or twelve o'clock and I decided to walk to Mr. Mercer's apartment.

I opened the door and went in. I smelled grilled sardines. The smell was good. I heard Mr. Mercer cursing. He was mad.

I asked him, "Why are you cussing?"

He said, "I hate the smell of sardines!"

"Did you ever have grilled sardines with wine? They're very good."

"No! I don't even like to look at sardines, and they smell awful!" Then he said to his secretary, "Are you ready? Let's leave. I don't want to smell those sardines any longer!"

They said, "Goodbye, Larbi," and they left. I stayed in the apartment and did my work. I finished earlier than the day before. I closed the door and I left.

The next day I came to work and I found Mr. Mercer and his secretary getting ready to leave. Then I heard the bell ring. I opened the door and there was a man standing there. He showed me a bottle of vodka that had been filled with honey.

He said, "This is honey. I'm selling honey."

He handed me the bottle and I touched it and it was still warm. I told him, "This is not honey. This is sugar, cooked sugar."

"Oh, no, no. I swear to Allah, this is honey."

"What kind of person do you think I am, that you want to sell me sugar for honey?"

"Oh, no, no. I'm not going to sell it to you. I'm going to sell it to the Europeans who live here."

"You think the Europeans are stupid like you and me? You think you're going to fool them—telling them this is honey? Take that bottle and go away." And I shut the door in his face. I went on doing my work.

Then I heard the bell ring again and finally I remembered seeing that man on the street. I had never known what he did for a living until that day he came to Mr. Mercer's apartment. I went and opened the door. It was the same, same man.

I said, "If you don't go away, I'm going to call the police and tell them you tried to cheat us."

"What's the matter with you? What kind of Moroccan are you? You're supposed to be on my side!"

"I don't think I can be on any thief's side when he tries to cheat somebody and I'm watching it."

We kept arguing back and forth and finally Mr. Mercer came out of his room and said, "What's wrong?"

I said, "Nothing. This man came by and he wanted to sell you sugar for honey. I can tell it's sugar because it's still warm. He just cooked it and brought it by."

He handed the bottle to Mr. Mercer and Mr. Mercer looked at it and I knew Mr. Mercer knew it wasn't honey. You couldn't put honey in a vodka bottle.

The man said, "Oh, no. It's honey. I don't think this man likes me, that's why he says it's not honey."

I kept telling Mr. Mercer not to buy it. I said, "Tell him to go away!"

Mr. Mercer asked him how much it was. He said it was 1,000 francs. Mr. Mercer pulled the money out of his pocket, took the bottle and put it on the dining room table. I closed the door and the man went away.

I knew Mr. Mercer bought the honey because he didn't want to hear me arguing with the man.

The following day I came to work. I opened the door, I went in and I looked at that bottle. It was already white and hard just as I thought it would be. I looked at it and I felt very sad about the whole thing. I took the bottle and

I put it in the garbage can.

I had worked one week. One afternoon Mr. Mercer said, "Larbi, we're going to Spain for two weeks. I want to pay you and you keep the key. Come back to the apartment from time to time and see if everything is all right."

I said, "I'll do that, Mr. Mercer."

When I came back the following day, their suitcases were already packed. Mr. Mercer called a taxi. I helped them put their suitcases in the taxi, I shook their hands and they left. I did my work as usual. I locked the apartment and I left. I didn't come back for four days. On the fifth day I decided to check the apartment. I told my wife I would be back in the afternoon. I walked all the way down to the Avenida de España. I opened the door and went in. I found a strange man in the apartment.

I asked him, "What are you doing here?"

He said, "I'm the owner of the house and I'm checking the apartment. Who are you? What are you doing here?"

"My name is Larbi and I work here for Mr. Mercer Saunders."

"I'm the Baron de Froisy, I'm the owner of the house. I live downstairs." Then he said, "I've never seen you here before."

"I've never seen you either. You have no right to come into people's apartments when they're not home. What kind of landlord are you? You know it's against the law to go into somebody's home when they're not here. How would you like me to go downstairs and snoop around your home without your knowing anything?"

"If you did that, I'd call the police!"

I saw he had some papers in his hand. I asked him where he'd found those papers.

He said, "Oh, I'm just looking at these papers."

"You're not supposed to touch anything or look at anything or move anything."

"You are the stupidest man I've ever known in my life! What's wrong with you?!" He stepped forward and slapped me. He began to scream. Then he started yelling, "Robber! Robber! Robber!"

I said, "I'm not a robber. You won't get away with that."

Then he went downstairs and called the police. He came back upstairs and said, "Don't run away! The police are coming. They're going to take you to jail."

"I'm not going to run away. I didn't do anything wrong."

"Oh, yes, you did! You came into the apartment without anyone knowing it."

"No. I have the key. You saw me. You were already here when I opened the door." I said, "Oh, no. You're the one who came into the apartment without anybody knowing it!"

"Well, we'll find out when the police come. Don't run away!"

"Ouakha. I'm going to be sitting right here."

The police came and the door was open. After they came in, the inspector asked me, "Are you the man who called the police?"

I said, "No. This man here was the one. He called you."

The Baron began talking. He introduced himself to the inspector. He told him he was the Baron. He said he was the one who owned the building and that he'd found me in the apartment.

I said, "That's not true! That's not true! I'm the one who found him in the apartment."

The inspector said, "Be quiet! Be quiet, you! I'll talk to you in a minute." I didn't say anything.

The inspector told one policeman to take Mr. Baron into the other room to take his statement. The inspector stayed with me. He said, "Tell me what happened."

"Mr. Inspector, I work for the man who lives in this apartment. His name is Mr. Mercer Saunders. He went away to Spain for two weeks and he gave me the key. He paid me for the two weeks. He told me to keep my eye on the apartment until he came back. But I'm still working for him. I came in this afternoon to check on the apartment and I found this man here in the apartment. I didn't know what he was doing here."

"Do you have any witnesses?"

"No, I don't have any witnesses." I put my hand in my pocket and I took out the key. "I have the key. Try it in the door. See how it fits."

The inspector took the key and put it in the lock and it worked. The other policeman came back from talking to the Baron and he was very excited. He told the inspector that I was definitely a thief.

I said, "No, Inspector! I'm not a thief!"

He said, "Be quiet! I told you to be quiet!" So I didn't say a word.

The inspector decided to call the authorities to find out who owned the building. He found out that the man owned the building.

The inspector said, "I know one of you is lying. The Baron owns the building, that's for sure." He said to me, "I have to take you in until we prove whether you're guilty or innocent."

"Inspector," I said, "I know how we can prove it. Let's go to the woman who got me the job. Her name is Lalla Ann. She can tell you that I'm working for Mr. Mercer."

"Where does this woman live?"

"She lives near the Spanish Consulate, on the other side of town."

"Are you sure about that — we can go up there and find out? You're not lying to me?"

"No, Inspector, I'm telling you the truth."

"Ouakha. We'll go up there." He said to the Baron, "Ouakha, now we have to leave. You go downstairs to your apartment, and we'll get in touch with you."

The Baron left, I closed the door and all of us left. I got into the jeep with the police and we drove through the town until we got to the Spanish Consulate.

The inspector said, "Where does the lady live?"

I said, "She lives down there in that tall building. I don't know the apartment number, but I know which one it is. She lives on the fifth floor."

We drove down in the jeep and they parked it in the garage. I rang the manager's bell and he opened the door. The manager asked the inspector if anything was wrong.

He said, "No, nothing is wrong. Does a woman named Ann live here?"

The manager said, "Yes. She lives on the fifth floor." Then he told us her apartment number.

We took the elevator to the fifth floor. We went to Lalla Ann's apartment and I rang the bell. The maid, Habiba, opened the door and she said, "What's wrong?"

I said, "I don't know. Is Lalla Ann home?"

She said, "Yes. Come in."

All three of us went in and we went into the living room.

Habiba said, "Sit down." We sat down on the cushions. Habiba went and told Lalla Ann that some people were looking for her. Lalla Ann came out and said, "Larbi, what's wrong?!"

The inspector said, "Don't say anything." He asked her, "Do you know this man?"

She said, "Yes, I know this man."

"Where do you know him from?"

"He used to work for some Americans who were friends of mine."

"What were their names?"

"One of them is John Redfield, he's a painter. The other's name is Richard Davis. He's a designer."

"This man claims you got him a job working for a man called Mr. Mercer Saunders."

"Yes, I'm the one who got him the job. I took him down and introduced him to Mr. Mercer Saunders." Then she asked the inspector, "What's wrong, Inspector? What happened?"

"There's nothing wrong. Whatever was wrong, we've cleared up now. I'm sorry we came and disturbed you. Will you please forgive us?"

"Of course, Inspector, I'm glad I could be of assistance to you."

The inspector gave me back the key. He said, "I'm sorry. We had to do our job." They left and I stayed there talking to Lalla Ann about what had happened between me and the Baron.

Lalla Ann said, "Oh, yes, I know the Baron doesn't like Mercer. A friend of Mercer's from New York leased the apartment from the Baron for two years. He's the one who is letting Mercer stay there. The Baron is angry because he isn't making any money from Mercer. Mercer didn't talk to him or ask his permission."

I told Lalla Ann, "When I came into the apartment, the Baron was looking at some papers. I don't know if he took anything or not. You should tell Mr. Mercer."

I left Lalla Ann's apartment. I went back home and I told my wife what happened. I said, "You almost didn't see me tonight. I was almost going to go to prison."

She asked me why. I said, "Never mind, it's a long story."

Then I asked her, "What would happen if I went to prison? What would you do?"

"I'd pick up my things and go to my mother's. I probably wouldn't even come to see you in prison."

"Well, that's a big help. I definitely can't count on you for anything." I asked her, "Do you have any dinner cooked?"

"Yes, I went to the market and I bought some fish. I cooked it with potatoes and tomatoes. Do you want to have dinner now?"

"Ouakha. I want to have dinner now and then I want to go to bed. I have to get up tomorrow morning and go to the port to look for work. I'm not making enough money now. Since you don't want to go to work, I can't depend on you."

She dished out the dinner and we ate and had tea. Then we went to bed. I got up early in the morning, as usual, and I went straight to the port. I kept asking if there was any work. There was one ship from Holland that needed to be unloaded. I got a job for that day, unloading the ship. It had a lot of heavy machinery to unload. I worked until noon, the whistle blew and we had an hour for lunch. At one o'clock the whistle blew and we went back to work. We worked until nine o'clock that evening. I made 5,000 francs that day. I said to myself, "This is a good day, not bad at all. If I work this way every day and make this much money, I don't have to worry about work. But jobs like this are hard to come by. You can usually only get one or two days a month."

I took my money and I went to the Zoco. It was very late. I took a taxi home. It cost me 500 francs to get home.

When I walked into the house, my wife said, "Why are you so late getting home?"

I said, "I worked all day long. I made lots of money."

"Show me the money. I don't believe you."

I took the money out and I gave her 5,000 francs. I knew that as soon as she got hold of money, she went straight to the jewelers to buy gold.

I went to bed. I said, "I don't want to talk about it anymore."

The following morning I got up and I left the house right away. I didn't even wash. I went to the mosque and I washed in the mosque. I stayed there for a while. About seven o'clock I went to the port to see if I could get some more work. I stayed there almost all day long. I didn't get any work. This afternoon I would go to my friend Mustafa's cafe and see how everyone was doing. I walked through the Medina until I got to my friend Mustafa's cafe. He was there. I said "Allah ihennik" and shook his hand.

He said, "Where have you been? I haven't seen you in a long time."

"Just here and there."

"If you'd been here this morning, you probably would have gotten work with that Jewish man. He needed someone to work unloading flour from trucks."

"I didn't know. I was sitting at the port all day, waiting to be called to work."

"Next time you go down to the port, you should see my brother. He's in charge of the ships when they come to unload. You should go see him. He usually sits in the

Administrator's office. That Jewish man can probably use more men in the morning, too."

Then he asked me, "Do you want to have tea?"

"Are you going to treat me, or do I have to pay for it?"

"Oh, no, you're my friend. I'll buy you a glass of tea."

"Well, sure, thank you."

He asked the qahouaji to make me a glass of tea. The qahouaji made the tea and said, "Ouakha, give me 20 francs."

I said, "Oh, no, Mustafa is going to pay for it."

Mustafa said, "Ouakha, put it in my account."

I stayed there talking to Mustafa for a while drinking tea until it was time to go home. Then Mustafa said, "I'm going home myself. I can give you a ride to my house and that will bring you closer to where you live."

I said, "Ouakha, I'll ride with you."

We went to Mustafa's car, he had a small Renault. I drove with him to his house, I got out and walked to my house, which wasn't very far. I opened the door and went in.

My wife said, "What happened to you? Did you get any work today?"

I said, "No."

"Why didn't you get a job? I bet everybody else got a job except you."

"No, I didn't get a job. I'm not the jefe who's in charge of jobs. I just wait there, and if there's jobs I get one, and if there's no jobs, I don't."

She said, "You have to work between tomorrow and the next day, because I'm going to go to a wedding and I need money to buy presents."

"I just gave you 5,000 francs yesterday. How could you spend that much money already?"

"I didn't spend that money, but I need more than that."

"What happened to the 10,000 francs I gave you three days ago?"

"I already spent the 10,000 francs."

"That quick? You spend money faster than anybody else I know! I'm sorry, I haven't any money. If I work, I'll give you some money. If I don't work, you run out of luck. Let's see how lucky you are. Now I'm going to bed, and I don't want to talk." I went straight to bed, without my dinner.

The following morning I got up; I washed and I dressed. My wife was still in bed; I didn't bother her. I didn't say anything to her. I left the house, went down to the Zoco to a restaurant and I asked for a bowl of soup and a half a loaf of bread. After I had breakfast, I decided to go to the apartment where I worked. I opened the door and I found a lot of mail under the door. I picked up the mail, and put it on Mr. Mercer's desk. There was a postcard with my name on it. I couldn't read the postcard. I decided to go see Lalla Ann. She would tell me what the postcard said. I walked through town to the building where Lalla Ann lived. I rang the manager's bell and he opened the door. He said, "I remember you. Aren't you the man who was here with the police?"

I said, "Yes, everything is all right. I just want to see Lalla Ann."

"Ouakha, go ahead."

I took the elevator to the fifth floor. I rang the bell and Habiba opened the door. She said, "It's you! What do you want this time?"

"I want to see Lalla Ann."

"Well, I don't think she wants to see you."

"Why don't you let her decide if she wants to see me

or not. Just tell her I'm here and that I want to see her."

"Ouakha, come in and sit down. I'll go see if Ann wants to see you."

I knew Habiba didn't like me to see Lalla Ann or to talk to Lalla Ann, but that was not my concern.

Lalla Ann came out from the other room. She said, "Good morning, Larbi."

I said, "Good morning, Lalla Ann."

"What can I do for you?"

"I found this postcard in Mr. Mercer's mail, and it has my name on it. I want to know what it says."

"Sure. Let me see." She read the postcard and she said, "It's from Mercer. He says he'll be home tomorrow or the day after tomorrow. He wants you to get the apartment ready for them when they come back."

"The apartment is all ready." I thanked Lalla Ann. I went back down to my friend Mustafa's cafe. I stayed there for a while, but the Jewish man never came looking for someone to work for him. It was late in the afternoon and I asked my friend Mustafa if I could borrow some money from him.

He said, "How much do you want to borrow?"

"5,000 francs. I'll pay you in two or three weeks."

"Sure, of course." He put his hand in his pocket and brought out 5,000 francs.

"Be sure to pay me in three weeks."

"Oh, sure. I'll pay you, if I don't die."

I left and went to the Soussi's. I bought three packs of cigarettes. The man took 60 francs. I walked and I walked, until I got home.

As soon as I opened the door, my wife jumped. She said, "Did you get any money? Did you work?"

I said, "No, I didn't work, but I got some money." I

took 4,000 francs out of my pocket and I gave them to her.

"4,000 francs is not enough to buy presents for the wedding."

"I'm sorry. If it's not enough, there's nothing I can do. If you want some more money, go out and get yourself a job and keep all the money you make."

"Why did you marry me if you can't support me?"

"Sweetheart, your habits are beyond my dreams! You spend money faster than I can make it."

She wasn't happy. She was very sad because that was all the money I could come up with that night. She said, "Think of what people will say—what kind of husband I married!"

"I don't care about what people will say. None of those people do anything for me—they don't pay my bills, they don't feed me, they don't take care of me. Why should I be concerned about those goddamn people? All they do is criticize other people. If you are so concerned about what people will say, why don't you go out and work? You'll have all that money for yourself. I promise I won't ask for a franc. You're not a princess like Lalla Aicha. Now you better be quiet. If 4,000 francs is not enough, that's tough luck!"

Two days later Mr. Mercer came back. I went to work.

I said, "Buenas tardes. How was your trip to Spain?"

He said, "Fine."

I told him about finding the Baron in the apartment, how he was looking through his papers.

He said, "Never mind the Baron! I'm leaving next week."

I told him I'd told Lalla Ann what happened, that she could probably explain it better than I could.

He said, "Fine. I'll talk to Ann."

The Baron started grilling his sardines again. I could see Mr. Mercer getting mad. He started mumbling about sardines.

I asked him if he wanted me to go down to the Baron and ask him not to grill sardines anymore.

"Oh, no, don't bother. I'm going to leave next week. The Baron already knows I don't like sardines. That's probably why he does it. He does it purposely." He said, "I'm going out now. Good afternoon. We'll see you tomorrow."

I said, "Ouakha."

They left and I stayed in the apartment. I did my work, as usual. I closed the door. I went home; my wife wasn't home. I decided she had gone to buy presents for the wedding. I felt very good when I found the house empty. I cooked my own dinner, I ate and I went to bed. My wife never came home that night.

I got up early in the morning. I washed and left. I went down to the Zoco Chico to see if I could find some of those people who unload contraband cigarettes from boats. I didn't find anybody who needed any help. I walked around for a while until about twelve o'clock. I went to work. Mr. Mercer and his secretary were just about to leave. I asked him if he had talked to Lalla Ann about the Baron.

He said, "Yes, I talked to Ann about the Baron. I don't know what he was looking for."

"Have you noticed any of your papers missing?"

"I don't know."

"If there's anything missing and you want me to go down and talk to him, I'd be glad to go. Because I'm very angry at him."

"Oh, no, no. Don't worry about him. In three days I'll be leaving, so it doesn't matter." And they left the apartment.

I began to talk to myself like a crazy person. I said to myself: "Every time I get a job, someone comes along and messes it up for me. Why? I know Allah will punish sinners but I wish Allah would punish the sinners *now.* I'll never see any justice." Then I said, "Oh, Allah, please forgive me. I'm angry. I don't know what I'm saying! I know your justice is the greatest justice man could ever have!"

I finished my work and I left. I stayed working for Mr. Mercer today and tomorrow. Three days later I came in one afternoon and Mr. Mercer said, "Larbi, we're leaving tomorrow afternoon about twelve-thirty. Our plane leaves at two o'clock. Will you please come a little earlier tomorrow?"

"What time do you want me to come?"

"Eleven o'clock will be fine."

"Ouakha, I'll be here tomorrow at eleven o'clock."

They left the apartment, the same as always, and I stayed there. I did my work, I finished earlier and I left. I went straight home. I found my wife at home.

I said, "Where were you last night?"

She said, "I spent the night at my sister's house. I was out late shopping and I didn't want to come home. I hadn't seen my sister for a long time."

"Don't you think you should tell me next time you want to spend the night out? With your sister or your mother or whoever you want to spend the night with?"

"You weren't home yesterday. That's why I didn't tell you."

"Show me the present you bought."

"I decided not to buy any present. I'm going to give the money instead of buying a present."

"Have you shopped for food?"

"No, I didn't shop for food. I just came from my sister's."

"What are we going to have for dinner?"

"Maybe I'll fry some potatoes."

"Ouakha. That'll be all right. Whatever you say."

She peeled some potatoes and cut them up and fried them. She put some tomato sauce on them and we had our dinner. I told her I was going to bed, I was very tired.

"So early? It's still so early."

"Yes, so early."

"Tomorrow night I won't be home. I'm going to go to the wedding. Then I'm going to go to my sister's and spend the night."

"Ouakha. That's all right. Do whatever you want. That's ouakha." And I went to bed.

The following morning I washed my face, and I left the house. I went straight to the beach and I went for a swim. I swam for a while. About ten-thirty I walked back to Mr. Mercer's apartment, I opened the door and I said "Buenos dias." I found them packing their things.

I said, "Can I help?" And they said, "No, We've almost got it all."

Mr. Mercer said, "Larbi, how much do I owe you?"

"Five days."

"All right, that's 5,000 francs. Here's 5,000 francs and here's 20,000 francs. This will make up for the time we're not going to be here. You've been so nice."

"Thank you very much. You've been even nicer to me than I was to you."

"Sure. Sure. Don't worry about it." Then he called a taxi and he said, "Here's what I want you to do. When we leave, I want you to pick up the two shopping bags and take them to Ann's."

A little bit later, the taxi came. I helped them carry their suitcases to the taxi. I shook their hands, and we said goodbye. And that was the last time I saw Mr. Mercer Saunders.

I went back to the apartment and I picked up the two

bags. I looked around. There wasn't anything else left in the apartment to take to Lalla Ann's. I saw a lot of loose change on the table. I put it all in the bottom of a bag. I closed the door and I left.

I walked about 100 yards down to the Avenida de España. A taxi came by and I told the driver I wanted to go to the Spanish Consulate. We drove up to Lalla Ann's building and I paid him 500 francs. I rang the manager's bell and I told him I had some things for Lalla Ann. He said, "Fine. Go ahead."

I put the two bags in the elevator and I went up to the fifth floor. Habiba opened the door and she said, "It's you again."

I said, "Yes, it's me again."

"How come you keep disturbing Ann all the time?"

"I'm not disturbing Lalla Ann all the time. I have some things here for her."

"Come on in, come on in, since you have something for her." She called Lalla Ann.

Lalla Ann said, "Ahilan, Larbi. What do you have?"

"Mr. Mercer wanted me to bring these two bags to you."

I put the bags down on the floor and I said, "Just a minute. The money down there belongs to me. Do you have a paper bag?"

She said, "Yes." She told Habiba, "Give him a paper bag," and she did.

I dumped all the loose change into the paper bag and I said, "This change belongs to me." I asked her, "What does Mr. Mercer do?"

"He writes books. He's a very, very famous writer in America."

"That's very good. I wish he had stayed here longer.

That was a very good job. Thank you for recommending me. I hope if you hear of any more jobs, you'll recommend me again." I shook her hand and I left. I stayed without work today and tomorrow. Sometimes I worked and sometimes I didn't work. The time went by until the summer of '63 when I went to work for Mr. Miles Weston.

2 / Journey to Arcila

I was home doing my gardening. I heard knocking on the door. I opened the door and there was Mr. Miles. I asked him what he wanted. "You never did come to see me. What do you want?"

He said, "I know you're not working right now. I'd hoped you'd like to work for me."

"Doing what?"

"You're going to be my houseboy."

"Ouakha."

"But," he said, "it's not going to be here in Tangier. It's going to be in Arcila."

"Ouakha. How much are you going to pay me?"

"I'll pay you 10,000 francs a week. $20.00. Get your things together. We leave the day after tomorrow. I'll come by at eleven o'clock and we'll go down to the Plaza de España."

"Ouakha. I'll be ready."

Two days later Mr. Miles came as he had said. I had my things all ready. I got into the taxi with him and we took off for the Plaza de España. By the time we got there, the bus we were supposed to take had already left. Then Mr. Miles said, "What a day! What bad luck. We'll have to go back home now."

"Just a minute. You don't mind if you ride with campesinos?"

"No, if we could get a bus."

"Ouakha. You wait here a minute. I'm going to those buses that take campesinos home and ask if they can take us with them to Arcila."

There were three buses loading people. I went to the driver and I asked him if he had room for two people. He said ouakha.

"Where are you two going?"

"We're going to Arcila. How much are you going to charge us?"

"You have to pay 700 francs each."

"Will you wait here? I'm going to get my friend."

I went back to where Mr. Miles was waiting. We picked up our suitcases and we walked to the bus. The driver said, "Oh, he's a Nazarene."

I said, "Yes, he's a Nazarene. Don't you take any Nazarene on your bus?"

"No, I never have before."

"You have nothing to worry about. My friend, he doesn't mind. He also speaks Moghrebi."

The bus driver said, "Ouakha. You two go in the back. There are two seats available."

We took our seats and I asked Mr. Miles to give me the money so I could pay the driver. I took the money and he said, "Now the bus is loaded. We're leaving right away."

He asked his helper if everything was ready. He closed the door. The bus took off. And we went along the mountain road.

Then Mr. Miles and I began to talk in Moghrebi. Everybody seemed surprised. Mr. Miles was speaking Moghrebi like a Moroccan. Two campesinos came up to us and they began to ask Mr. Miles questions. They had doubts that Mr. Miles had spoken Moghrebi, but he answered their questions. They began to offer us food and wine. I started eating with them. They offered me wine. I said, "No. I don't drink." They offered Mr. Miles wine and he said no, he didn't want any.

One campesino said, "How come you don't drink? You're a Nazarene and you don't drink."

Mr. Miles said, "I don't drink because I have liver trouble."

The campesino said, "Ouakha. If you are sick, you don't drink."

The same campesino asked me, "Would you like to change places with me?"

I said: "Ouakha." I went and sat with the campesino's sister. He sat with Mr. Miles because he found him very interesting. He had never in his life spoken Moghrebi with a Nazarene.

I asked the campesino's sister where she lived.

"We live in Hajra den Nhal."

"What is your name?"

"Aicha."

"Aicha, do you ever come to Arcila?"

"Yes, sometimes."

"You should come and see me sometime. I'm going to be working in Arcila."

The bus kept going up in the mountains on the winding

road. We finally got to the village called Hajra den Nhal. All the people that had to get off there did get off, and the bus was half full then. I went back to my seat with Mr. Miles and I sat there with him. Then one campesino brought out a guinbri from his sack and he began to play music. Everybody else joined and we all began to clap our hands. Everybody was having a good time on the bus. The campesinos' bus turned out to be a good ride.

We got to Arcila. The driver called, "Everybody out. This is the end of the line."

I asked Mr. Miles, "Where is the house?"

"The house is inside the Medina. We have to take a taxi to get there."

We took a taxi and we went through the Medina until we got to a big palace by the cliffs of Arcila. We passed the palace. The house was further up to the right. We reached the house; inside it was very nice.

I asked Mr. Miles, "Who does this house belong to?"

"It belongs to a Spanish general. I rented it from him. You take the room under mine. Ann will take the room upstairs across from mine."

"My room looks very small."

"This is all that is available."

The room was a triangle and had a small window looking out to the sea. It was no bigger than eight feet by six feet. The door was right next to the front door of the house. I picked up the suitcases and I took them upstairs to Mr. Miles's room. When I came back downstairs Mr. Miles said, "Now we need a maid."

I said, "I don't know anybody in Arcila. Why don't you go and see the man who rented you the house. He might know some lady who wants to work."

"I'll do that tomorrow morning."

The next day we had our breakfast. I told Mr. Miles, "Now we should go see the man about the maid." We walked through the Medina to the other side of town. When we got to the house, I knocked on the door. A man came out. Mr. Miles told him that he needed a maid.

The man said, "Ouakha. I know a woman named Fatoma. She isn't working right now. She may work for you."

We went back to the house. We waited for a while. Then the man came to the door. He had a woman with him. The man introduced her to Mr. Miles: "Her name is Fatoma. She wants to work."

Fatoma asked Mr. Miles how much he would pay her.

He said, "I'll pay you 500 francs a day. You'll work from eleven in the morning to three in the afternoon."

She asked, "Can I start today?" He said she could.

Mr. Miles began to show her the rooms and everything else.

A little bit later I locked the house and I went to the market. I bought the food we would need. That was my job: to go shopping and to keep an eye on the house.

We stayed there today and tomorrow. One afternoon I was sitting on the roof and I heard dogs barking. I went to look. I saw this strange man I had never seen before. He had two dogs with him.

He asked me, "Do you know a man named Miles Weston—where he lives?" He spoke to me in Spanish.

"Yes. He lives right here in this house. My name is Larbi."

"My name is Haskell Josephs. I know who you are. I'm here to write a book, and I would like to write a story about you."

"That will be fine. Whenever you are ready."

Then Mr. Miles came back. I said: "This is Mr. Haskell. He is looking for you."

Mr. Miles said, "Oh, yes. I've been expecting you." He asked Haskell to come into the house.

I helped Haskell with his luggage and his two dogs. He asked me if I knew of a house for rent.

I said, "I don't know. I'll have to go out and look."

I went out into the neighborhood and I began to ask people if they knew of a house for rent. I asked a man three houses from our house. He said yes, his house was for rent.

I told him a man who came from America was looking for a house. I said, "Wait a minute. I'm going to go get him."

I went back to our house and I told Haskell, "I found a house for you."

He said, "Where is it?"

"It is the third house down from ours." I took him to the house. I introduced him to the man who owned the house.

Haskell said, "Yes, I like it. How much do you want for a month?"

He said, "It will cost you 25,000 francs ($50) a month. That will include the utilities."

"Fine. I'll take it."

He rented the house and I helped him carry his luggage.

I told Haskell, "Now, if you want to go downtown and buy some things you need for the house, I'll be glad to go with you."

We walked through the Medina until we got downtown. There was a Jew who owned a hardware store.

Haskell began to collect things he needed. I told him, "Now you have the house and things you need. If you need anything else, come to my house. We'll go get it."

I stayed there working for Mr. Miles, today and tomorrow. About a week later I said to myself, Right now I'm not doing very much. I think from now on, every Thursday and Sunday, I'm going to go up to the campesinos' market in Hajra den Nhal and I'll start buying silver coins. I can make jewelry.

I started going up to the campesinos' market, as I planned. I began to buy silver coins until I collected about two hundred pieces. Then I began to make necklaces and earrings with them.

One afternoon two men came looking for Mr. Miles. Mr. Miles wasn't home. I told the two men to come back later. Mr. Miles came back home and I told him there were two men looking for him.

He said, "Do you know who they are?"

"No. I don't."

A little bit later the same two men came back. They knocked and I opened the door. I called Mr. Miles. I said, "Those two men, they're here."

I let them in. They went to the dining room and sat along the big, long table. I asked them if they wanted any tea. They said yes. I made a big pot of tea and I gave it to them. I gave them cups. They poured their own tea. They began to talk. They asked Mr. Miles if they could spend the night in the house. He said, "No. Nobody spends the night in my house."

I said, "Why don't we let them spend the night in the guest house on the other side of the palace? It's empty all the time."

"If they want to spend the night over there, it's all right with me."

After a while they finished their tea. I told them, "Will you come with me, and I'll show you the house." I got the key and took them to the house. I showed it to them. They said they wouldn't mind spending the night there.

One room had a big straw mat. I said, "It gets very cold at night." They said they didn't mind. "It's better than sleeping outside."

I said, "Tonight I'll let you have two of my blankets. You men won't be so cold."

They said, "Now we're going to go for a walk through the Medina. It looks very interesting. At night we'll come back to your house so you'll give us the blankets and the key."

They went away and I went back to our house. I asked Mr. Miles why he didn't let them sleep in the house since half of it was empty.

He said, "I don't know these men. I've never seen them before."

"They didn't really want anything. All they wanted was to spend the night. That wouldn't be hard to do."

"Goddamnit! This is my house, and don't tell me how to run it!"

I went out to the beach to see if I could buy some fresh fish but I didn't find any. They had already sold everything. I was a little too late. I went back to the Medina and I started walking around. I ran into the same two men I'd talked to earlier. I asked them how come they came to Morocco without any money. One of them said, "We have money!"

I said, "Why don't you men take a hotel room?"

The same one who said they had money said, "We'd like to save our money because we're going for a trip around the world."

Then I asked them where they were going on their next trip. They said, "On our next trip we're going to go to Spain."

I said, "Which part of Spain are you going to?"

"We're going to Madrid."

I said, "I know there are a lot of tourist shops in Madrid. I've been making some jewelry for a while—can you men take my jewelry to Madrid and sell it and send me the money?"

"Oh, yes. We'll be glad to do that for you because you've been very good to us."

"No, I didn't really do anything for you."

They said, "Oh, yes, you did a lot. If it wasn't for you, we would probably be sleeping in the street tonight."

"Don't worry about it. Don't even mention it. Now it's getting late. Why don't you two come with me so I can give you the key and the blankets. You can go to sleep whenever you want to."

We walked back to the house. I gave them the key and the blankets. I told them, "We'll see you in the morning."

I closed the door and went back to my room. I slept until morning. I got up in the early morning. I found the two men already waiting for me at the door. I asked them how they had slept. They said, "It was pretty good."

I let them in and I told them to sit down. I was going to make tea. I made a pot of tea and I toasted a loaf of bread. I put some butter and honey on the bread. And the three of us had breakfast.

We finished our breakfast and I took the dishes back to the kitchen. The two men said, "Now we are going to leave. We have to go to the bus station to get the bus back to Tangier. And you had something for us you wanted us to take to Spain for you."

I went back to my room and I got the basket. I put the basket on the table and I took out all the jewelry I had made. I told them, "This is what I have made. There are twenty-four necklaces and twenty-four earrings. I am going to keep four of both and give you the twenty to take with you to Spain." I wrapped the twenty necklaces in a piece of cloth, and I gave them the bundle. I told them, "Please, whatever you do with them, or whatever happens to them, write me a letter. And when you sell them, send me the money."

Mr. Miles came downstairs. He said good morning to them. They answered back. Then he asked them where they were going.

They said, "Right now we are going to Tangier. And we thank you very much for letting us spend the night at the other house."

He said, "That was nothing."

And they said, "Goodbye," and left.

One week later Lalla Ann was coming to Arcila for the first time. Mr. Miles told me, "Tomorrow Ann is going to be here at eleven o'clock and you have to go meet her at the bus station."

"Why don't you come with me? It will make Lalla Ann feel good."

"I'm going to be busy."

"Ouakha. I'll do it."

The next day I left the house on the way to the station. Haskell was walking his dogs and he said, "Good morning, Larbi."

I said, "Good morning, Haskell."

"Where are you going?"

I said I was going to the bus station to meet Lalla Ann. "She's coming today."

"Can I go with you? I know Ann would be very happy to see me. Why isn't Miles going with you to meet Ann?"

"He is very busy."

We walked through the Medina, and we had a little trouble with the children throwing stones at the dogs. I told them to go away, to leave us alone. The children, they kept coming after us. I told Haskell to let his dogs loose, to take their chains off. Haskell took the chains off and the dogs began to chase the children. Finally, by the time we got to the station there weren't any more children following us.

A few minutes later the bus came and we saw Lalla Ann. She was sitting in the bus with the maid called Meriam. Meriam was the maid who worked for Lalla Ann in Tangier. They stepped out of the bus. Then I picked up the suitcase and big basket and I said to the two ladies, "Welcome to Arcila."

Lalla Ann said, "I've been through Arcila so many times, but I've never lived in it."

Haskell held Lalla Ann's hand and we started walking toward the house. Then Lalla Ann asked me, "Why didn't Mr. Miles come?" I told her he was busy.

We kept walking until we got to the house. I opened the door and I took Lalla Ann to her room.

She said, "This room is beautiful." And Mr. Miles came walking up the stairs. He kissed Lalla Ann and asked her how her trip had been. She said it was pretty good. Then Haskell asked Ann if she wanted to go with him tomorrow to the beach.

I told them, "Now I'm going to go out for a walk." I went downtown to a cafe and I ordered a glass of tea. I sat there drinking tea.

3 / The Watermelons

A truck full of watermelons came up and stalled in front of the cafe. I finished my tea. I walked over to the truck. I asked the driver what was wrong. He said he didn't know. Something was wrong with it. I said to myself, Maybe I should go into the watermelon business. That will keep me busy. I asked the driver if he was selling the watermelons.

He said, "Yes. This is the man who owns the watermelons. Why don't you talk to him?"

I started talking with the man who owned the watermelons. We started bargaining about the price. He asked for 100,000 francs. I offered him 40,000. We kept bargaining for a little while and finally we came to an agreement. I gave him 60,000 francs ($120) for the whole truckload. We shook hands and the deal was made. I told the owner, "Now you bring the truck and come with me. We have to take it to the market."

We drove the truck to the market, which wasn't very

far, about half a mile away to the west.

When we go there I told the men, "This is the corner where we are going to put the watermelons. You start unloading the watermelons, I'm going home to get you the money."

He said, "Oh, no, I'd like to have the money before I take one watermelon out of my truck."

"Don't you trust me?"

"No! I don't know you. How can I trust you?"

"You wait here until I come back."

"How long is it going to take?"

"It will take about 10 or 15 minutes."

I ran home. I had 30,000 francs. I told Mr. Miles, "I bought a truckload of watermelons and I need 30,000 francs ($60) from you. You can take it a little bit at a time out of my salary each week."

He said, "If you are going to be selling watermelons, how are you going to work for me?"

"Don't worry. With Allah's help, I can do everything!"

He gave me the money and I went back. I paid the man for his watermelons. I told them to start unloading the watermelons and I'd be back soon. I went back to my neighbor, Latif. I asked him if he wanted to go partners with me on a watermelon truck.

He said, "Yes. But I don't have any money."

I told him he didn't need any money because I'd already paid for the watermelons. He said "Ouakha."

I said, "Good. Come with me. There are some people unloading the truck."

Latif and I walked back to the market. We got to the truck and we started helping the other men unload the truck. It took us about two hours. Finally we unloaded it. I told Latif, "We need one more person."

He said, "I know a man named Taib. He's not working. He probably will be interested."

"Why don't you go and see if you can find him at home."

He left. A little bit later he came back with another man I didn't know. He introduced me to him and said, "He's interested in working with us."

I said, "Here's the way we're going to do it. Whatever profit we make we are going to split it in three parts. Do you two agree?"

They said, "Ouakha. We agree."

I said, "Now let's try these watermelons and see how sweet they are. Latif, you slice one watermelon for us."

We tried the watermelon and it was the best watermelon anyone had ever sold in Arcila. It was very, very sweet. And they said, "Umm. This is pretty good!"

Latif asked me how much we were going to sell the watermelons per kilo. I said, "We should sell them for 15 francs, 3¢, a kilo. Now we have to arrange the schedules so somebody will be here all the time. And we need a scale. We don't have one."

Latif said, "You see that store out in front of us? That man rents scales."

I walked across the street and rented a scale for 100 francs a day. I brought back the scale. I told the two men, "Now I'm going to go home. I'll be back late tonight so you two can go home."

I walked home. I found Lalla Ann and Meriam cooking dinner. Lalla Ann asked me, "Where are your watermelons?"

I said, "They're in the market."

She asked me, "Are we going to have a watermelon from the watermelons you bought?"

"Ouakha. I'm going back to get one watermelon and we'll have it with dinner."

I went back to the market, picked out the biggest atermelon and brought it home. We had our dinner and Lalla Ann began to talk about how big a businessman I was. I said, "Oh, yes, I'm a big shot now!" And she laughed. I told her, "Tomorrow is Thursday. The market is going to be full. I want you to come over there and talk to me."

She said, "Oh, yes. Tomorrow we have to come anyway; we have to buy some things to take to Tangier with us."

We finished our dinner and I helped pick up the dishes. I asked Lalla Ann, "Are you ready for a feast of watermelon?" I went to the kitchen and I brought a big knife and a big plate. And I cut the watermelon in half. I sliced the half in small pieces. We tasted that watermelon. It was sweet, much as the first one was. Everybody had a taste and they gave me many compliments about how good a watermelon it was. I said, "I'm glad you all like my watermelon."

Lalla Ann said, "When I go back to Tangier, I'm going to buy some watermelons from you."

I said, "That won't be necessry. You can have one watermelon to take with you. Now I'm going to get some things to sleep on. I'm going to spend the night with the watermelons."

I picked up two blankets and a pillow, and I went back to the market. When I got to the market, my partners had already sold 5,000 francs worth of watermelons. I said, "This is a good start! Not so bad, not so bad at all." I told the two men now they could go home and come back in the morning. I told them to take one watermelon each for their families.

They left and I stayed. I picked up some watermelons from the center of the pile to make enough room for me to sleep. I spread my blanket in the center, put a pillow in there and lay down. I went to sleep until early morning. I heard chickens, donkeys and people coming from all over. I saw there were a lot of people in the market. It was almost full. The campesinos began asking me how much the watermelons were. I told them fifteen francs a kilo.

One lady said, "Are you selling the watermelons with proof?"

I said, "Yes, ma'am, I am selling them all with proof. If it's not sweet, I don't want you to buy it."

She said, "Ouakha. I want to buy two watermelons from you, but I want you to give me the proof."

"Ouakha. Will you please pick out the two watermelons you like."

She picked up two and I put them, one by one, in the scale. And they weighed 21 kilos, both of them. She said, "Now, I want to taste the proof."

I took a knife and I made a little square. I picked it out and gave it to her to taste. She had a taste and she liked the watermelon. She said, "Pretty good, pretty good." All of a sudden, I had too much business. I didn't even know how to handle it.

A little bit later my two partners came. I told them, "Now I'm going to leave. You two take care of it."

I went home and I found breakfast already made. Lalla Ann and Meriam had got up earlier. Lalla Ann asked me how I had slept out there.

I said, "Pretty good."

"Did you get cold?"

"No. It was very pleasant."

"What are you going to do today?"

"As soon as I have my breakfast, I am going to go back to help my partners. The market is full of people already."

I had my breakfast and I told Meriam that if they needed me for anything, I would be out in the market. Lalla Ann said, "We are going to go to the market, Meriam and I, pretty soon. We want to see Arcila's market. How is it?"

"It's pretty good. Now I'm going, we'll see you later."

I walked back to the market and it was full. There wasn't even space for anybody to walk around. I stepped into the middle of the watermelons and I started helping my partners. A little bit later I heard Haskell and Lalla Ann talking together. They weren't very far away from where I was. They got to where I had my business. Lalla Ann said, "All these watermelons belong tc you?"

I said, "Yes, to me and these two men."

Lalla Ann told Meriam, "Look how many watermelons Larbi has. He could feed a whole army with them."

Meriam said, "Yes, Larbi now is a big businessman."

Lalla Ann said to Meriam, "Come on now. We have to go and see what we are going to buy for our house in Tangier."

They went away and we were surrounded by people. Then Haskell asked me to pick out one good watermelon for him. I told him, "I'm not very lucky picking out things for other people. Why don't you pick one out, perhaps you'll be luckier than I." Haskell picked out a watermelon and I said, "Would you like to try it?"

He said, "No, I don't have to. If it's not good, I'll bring it back to you. How much is it?"

"Give me 500 francs."

"This watermelon looks very heavy."

"That's all right. Give me 500 francs and that's it."

He asked me, "What time are you not very busy?"

"In the afternoon is the best time. We don't have much business in the afternoon."

He said, "I want to ask you some things."

Meriam brought a big basket full of food and left it with us. She went back to where Lalla Ann was waiting for her. Haskell paid me, took his watermelon and went home.

A little bit later Lalla Ann and Meriam came back with two other baskets full of food. Lalla Ann said, "Now I'm very tired. I would like to sit down for a little while." I went to the cafe and I got her a chair. She sat down and we began to talk about how much food she had bought. She said, "I'm going to give some of this food to the other maid in Tangier who has a lot of cousins and nieces."

Meriam took a basket of food and said, "I'm going to the house."

I said, "Go ahead, and when Lalla Ann rests I will bring this food and walk with her to the house."

Lalla Ann and I, we kept talking, and a little bit later two country women came to where the business was. They remembered Lalla Ann; she had bought some peanuts from them. I said, "What can I do for you ladies?"

They said, "We came back to talk with this sweet lady. We've never met anybody like her who can speak Moghrebi like we do." The two women sat down on the low wall.

I said, "Ladies, since you are now going to be talking and having all sorts of conversation, how about letting me treat you to some tea or coffee to drink?"

Then the two women said, "Ouakha, we would like to have some tea." And Lalla Ann wanted some too.

"Now you ladies go ahead with your conversation and I'll be back in a minute." I went to the cafe and I asked the qahouaji to make us six glasses of tea and bring them to the watermelon pile.

I walked back. I found some other women there, too. They all surrounded Lalla Ann. She was talking in Moghrebi and they were very excited listening to her. I said, "What's this, ladies? You are all crowding my business place. What's going on?"

Lalla Ann said, "You be quiet. You men are all alike!" And all the women began to laugh. They laughed and laughed because the way she said it, it sounded just like a Moroccan woman.

My corner of the market got more and more crowded. All those women wanted to listen to Lalla Ann speak in Moghrebi. One of the women told Lalla Ann, "You should be telling stories in the market, like men do." Finally the tea arrived.

I said, "Here's the tea, ladies. I only ordered six glasses. I think some of you have to share the tea."

They laughed, "Of course we are going to share the tea! What do you think we are?"

"Ouakha, ladies, take care of yourselves."

I looked at Lalla Ann. She was very pleased and very, very happy. She was having such a good time. Then this Jewish man stepped in. He asked my partner to tell him how much he was selling the watermelons for. The Jewish man said, "No. This is too much. People are selling watermelons for five francs or ten, no more than twelve francs."

Taib said, "We sell them for fifteen francs for everybody, and you can take all the watermelons you want."

The Jewish man said, "No. I'm going to see what I can find. See all those watermelons? They are sold cheaper than yours."

My partner said, "Ouakha. If you can find a

watermelon like this, go ahead and buy it." The man left.

I heard one of the women inviting Lalla Ann to come to Hajra den Nhal on the Sunday after next. "We are going to have a wedding and we would like to invite you so you could talk to a lot of the ladies in the village."

Lalla Ann said, "Ouakha, I would like to come." Lalla Ann asked her how was she going to get to the village.

The woman said, "The bus leaves Arcila late Sunday. You take it to the village and we will bring an extra horse for you, and pick you up from there."

"I don't know how to ride a horse."

"You will have no problem riding a horse. You didn't have any problem learning Moghrebi. Now we're going to leave; it's getting late."

The women left and Lalla Ann said, "I would like to go home." I picked up the two baskets full of food and we walked to the house. I gave the two baskets to Meriam.

I walked back and I told my two partners, "Now we don't have very much business. Why don't you two go home and come back later so I can go home myself."

Finally the qahouaji came back to pick up his glasses. He said, "I've heard everyone talking about your watermelons. They are very sweet. I'd like to try one myself."

"Why don't you pick out a watermelon, and we will call it a fair trade. You gave me six glasses of tea and I give you a watermelon."

He said, "Ouakha." He picked out a watermelon, picked up his glasses and left.

The Jewish man came back. He asked me, "What happened to the other two men that were here?"

"They left, and they'll be back later. What can I do for you?"

"I would like to buy a watermelon from you, but you are asking too much money."

"No. I think fifteen francs is a fair price. I sold so many watermelons today I couldn't even handle the business, and you are telling me it's too much?"

"I'll give you twelve francs a kilo and I would like to buy two watermelons from you today."

"No. I don't think you are I are going to do any business."

"Ahmed, you look very stubborn."

"No, I'm not stubborn. I just like to sell the watermelons for the same price."

I kept saying no and he kept saying yes. He finally persuaded me to sell him the watermelons for thirteen francs. I told him not to tell my partners I sold the watermelons for this price, or they would get very mad at me.

"Oh, no! I swear I won't do that!"

He started picking up watermelons, one by one, one by one. I said, "That is not going to tell you anything, if you keep picking up the watermelons. They're all good and they all taste sweet."

"I know more about watermelons than you do. I've been buying watermelons all my life."

"Ouakha, probably."

He finally picked out two watermelons. I said, "Are you sure those two, they're going to be all right?"

"You still have to sell them to me with proof. If I taste them and they aren't sweet, I'm not going to pay you for them."

I took a knife, opened up the two watermelons and took a piece out of each of them. He tasted them and said, "Ouakha." He paid me, picked up his watermelons and left.

A little bit later Haskell came over. He began to ask me questions about the book. We talked for a while and my partners came. I asked Haskell if he would like to go to the beach to see if there were any fresh fish to buy. He said, "That's a good idea."

We walked toward the beach, which wasn't very far. There were all kinds of people selling fish; that was the time of day the boats came in. I bought some fish and Haskell did too. And we walked back to the house. Then Haskell said, "Well, I'll probably see you later if you are going to spend the night at the market."

I said, "Ouakha." I opened the door and Lalla Ann was there. She said, "Where did you get all the fish? They look good. What are you going to do with them?"

"I got them down by the beach. I'm going to clean them and let Meriam fix them for tomorrow."

I cleaned the fish and put them in the pot and gave it to Meriam. I walked to the table and it was covered with a cloth. I lifted up the cloth and there were all kinds of food on the table. I said, "Who is going to eat all this food?"

She said, "Tomorrow we are going to have some guests coming from Tangier."

"Is there anybody I know?"

"Probably. There are two French ladies who own a bookstore and a French doctor."

"How long are they going to stay here?"

"Oh, they are only coming to visit for tomorrow."

"That's good." I had two sandwiches and I left the house.

4 / This Is My Niece Lila

I went back to the market. I stayed there with my partners, talking about who had the best watermelons in town. I saw two women. It was Fatoma, the maid who lived in Arcila, and another younger woman with her. Fatoma called me. She said, "Come over here. We want to talk to you." When I got to them, she introduced me to the young girl. She said, "This is my niece, Lila."

I shook her hand and Lila said, "I would like to come and spend some time with you. I would like you to take me out to the cinema."

"What do you want with me? Don't you know I'm already married?" She said that Fatoma told her I hadn't seen my wife since I'd been in Arcila.

"Well, it doesn't really matter. If I want to see my wife, all I have to do is write her to come. At the moment, I don't like to be with anybody. I don't like to be with anybody because I already have enough trouble with my wife as it is."

She said, "Well, I just want you to know, if you ever want to go out with me you just have to tell Fatoma and I'll know about it."

I said, "Allah ihennikoum." I went back to the business.

My partners asked me what those two women wanted with me. I said, "Nothing, nothing. You men take care of things."

I went to the Medina where there is a big copper gun which was brought by the Spanish. I heard some people talking about the gun. It was a legend. One time a man brought a saw and started cutting off a piece of the gun so he could sell it for copper. The gun began to cry. Nobody could explain the mystery of the gun. The man stopped cutting the copper gun and his saw was broken in pieces. Nobody knew why. I didn't believe the story. I kept asking different people about it and everybody told me the same thing. I saw the cut with my own eyes. It was deep in the gun, about an inch down. I left and I wondered about the whole story, if it was true or if it wasn't.

I went back to the market, and I asked my two partners the same thing about the gun: if they knew what had happened to it and why it had a cut in it. They told me the same story. One of my partners said, "About ten years ago they caught three men trying to steal the gun. They had tied the gun to a truck with a chain and pulled, but they couldn't move the gun one inch. The truck broke and was lit on fire. That's why we call it the legendary gun. And that's why the robbers were caught. I think that gun is being watched by someone, from beyond this world."

It was getting late and I told my two partners, "I'm going to go home and have my dinner."

I went home and I asked Meriam if she had any dinner cooked. She said, "Yes. Ann made a big pot of food. Go to the kitchen and help yourself." I went in and I picked up a plate and filled it with food.

I ate and ate. The more I ate the better the food tasted. I asked Meriam, "Where is Lalla Ann? I must thank her for this nice dinner she cooked."

She said, "She is sitting on the roof with Mr. Miles."

I walked up to the roof and I said, "Lalla Ann, that was a good dinner."

She said, "I'm glad you liked it. I thought we'd probably have some left and we were going to leave it for you."

I said, "Thank you," and I left.

When I got to Haskell's house, there were some children chasing his dogs. That was one thing that made Haskell very upset, when the children chased his dogs. Of course, there aren't many Moroccans who like dogs. That's why the children chased the dogs.

I walked back to the market. I told my partners now they could go home if they wanted. My partners went home and I spent the night there as usual.

The next day, early in the morning, Haskell came by. He said, "Good morning, Larbi." I said, "Good morning, Haskell." Haskell asked if I had any time to talk to him this morning. I said: "Ouakha." He sat down and we began to talk. A little bit later, my two partners came back. I told Haskell, "I'm going down to the beach. If you want to keep talking to me, come with me."

We started walking through the Medina. We saw Lalla Ann. She was on her way to the beach. I said, "Good morning, Lalla Ann, it looks like you're up early this morning."

She said, "I want to go to the beach before my guests come." Then she asked if I was going to have breakfast. I said I wasn't hungry. Haskell said that it was a good thing Ann came along. We walked, all three of us, until we got to the beach. Haskell didn't ask me any more questions. We walked quietly for a long distance. Lalla Ann said she was tired and wanted to go back home. We walked all the way back home.

I said to myself, I think today I'll walk up on the wall that surrounds Arcila.

I started from where we lived and I walked along the wall all the way to the market. I was standing on top of the wall when I saw my partner Taib. I saw him take some money out of the business and put it in his son's basket. Then he put one watermelon on top of the money and told his son to take the basket home. There I was, watching everything. I jumped down and asked Taib what happened to Latif. He said Latif went home; his wife wanted him.

"How's the business?" I asked.

He said, "Pretty good."

I asked him how much money he made on sales.

"7,000 francs."

"That's not bad. Did you take any money from it?"

"No, I didn't take any of it."

"Are you sure your son wasn't here, and you gave him some money from our business?"

"I'm sure. No, no, I didn't give any money to my son."

I felt very sad about the whole thing, because I saw him with my own eyes put money in a basket, and he denied it. I thought about how I hoped I would make back the money I spent for those watermelons. Finally Latif came back and said, "How are we all doing today?"

I said, "Fine, fine."

I stayed there for a while, with the two of them. I saw a taxi coming toward the market. It was full of people. I rmemembered the two French ladies and the French doctor. They stopped the car and asked me where Mr. Miles's house was. I said, "Come, I'll show you."

There were three other people there whom I didn't know. They asked if we could walk from where we were. I said, "Yes."

We walked through the Medina until we got to the house. I opened the door and let them in. I called Lalla Ann and told her the guests had arrived. She came downstairs and they introduced each other. Of course, she knew the two French ladies and the doctor.

I left the house and went back to the market. I stayed there with my two partners for a while. I decided on my own that I wouldn't tell my other partner about Taib's stealing the money. Latif said, "Do you remember the two ladies who came looking for you the other day? We asked you who they were. You didn't answer."

I told Latif, "To be honest with you, the older lady's name is Fatoma. She's a maid who works where I work. The younger one's name is Lila, and I've never seen her before."

He said, "I know that young lady, she goes out with a lot of different men."

"You're trying to tell me she's a whore."

"Yes, exactly."

"I don't think that's my problem at all. Let's change the conversation to something else."

Latif said, "Do you want tea? I'm buying today."

I told him he didn't have to buy anything since we had plenty of money from our business. I said I was going to the cafe to get tea.

When I got back, I found that same Jewish man arguing with my partners about the price of the watermelons I had sold him before. My two partners asked why I had sold this man watermelons cheaper than I had sold them to anybody else. They said we agreed to sell watermelons at the same price to everybody.

I apologized to them and said, "I'm sorry. You two can take the difference out of my share."

"But that's not the point," they said. "You have to tell us why you sold him the watermelons cheaper."

The man saw us all arguing and left. I told my partners that he's probably a better businessman than me, his words sounded very persuasive and I couldn't persuade him to buy the watermelons for the same price as everyone else.

Taib said, "Don't you know that he's the richest man in Arcila?"

"No, I didn't know that. Even if I had, it wouldn't have made any difference to me." I finally realized it wasn't such a good day at all.

I told my partner Latif, "I'm going to go up to the woods."

I walked for a long distance until I got to the woods. I stayed there for a while. I started thinking about my partner, Taib. And I thought, How could he steal our money? Probably because he didn't put any money into the business. I said to myself, money stolen never lasts for long.

I walked down to the beach. I was feeling a little better. I ran into the same girl, Lila, and she said, "Ahilan, what happened to you the other day? You wouldn't even talk to me in the market."

"I didn't talk to you because I didn't want to have anything to do with you."

"What's the matter, don't you think I'm beautiful?"

"Oh, yes, you are very beautiful, but you should see my wife, how beautiful she is. Beauty is not in the way a person looks. Beauty is in a person's soul. That's why I got this job thirty miles away from my wife, because she is so beautiful."

"Don't get upset. I just want to let you know, if you ever want to be with me, you are free to do so."

"I don't really think I want to be with you, so please don't bother me any more."

"You know, there isn't a man in Arcila who would reject me."

"Ouakha. Why don't you go and look for those men. Right now, you see, these people are watching us. They might think we have something to do with one another. Please go away and don't follow me any more."

I walked down to the beach. I was getting hungry.

I went home and I found there were a lot of people in the house. I asked Meriam if she had any food left. She said, "Oh, yes. There's plenty of food on the table. Go help yourself." I went to the table and I helped myself.

Then I saw the lady doctor and I remembered her from the day when I took my baby to see her. I had found a lot of people in her office. She was treating them free of charge. Nobody had to pay any money. That's how I remembered that wonderful lady. The doctor asked me, "Larbi, are you going to stay here for a while? Don't you remember me?"

I said, "Yes, madame, I remember you very well. Thank you very much for helping my baby. Now I'm going to the market. I want you on your way back to Tangier to stop by and I'll give you a watermelon to take back with you."

"Oh, yes, I heard about your sweet watermelons. Ann said they were so wonderful. I'd like to come and take one back with me."

I said, "Allah ihennik. Don't you forget to come by the market."

I left the house. On the way back to the market, I found Haskell talking to a man.

He introduced me to the man: "This is Driss." Driss told me he was trying to explain to Haskell how he had had an accident on the boat and broken his leg. He could hardly walk. Haskell told him if he could get a passport, he would take him to London and he could have an operation on his leg. Haskell told him that he wanted to talk to his boss about his accident.

Driss said, "Tomorrow about two-thirty or three o'clock, you come down to the beach and there will be all the boats coming from fishing. I work on a tuna boat. There's where this accident happened to me. My boss will be there, and you can talk to him."

I asked Haskell if he understood everything. He said, "Yes. I want you to come with me tomorrow so we can talk to his boss."

I said, "Ouakha. I'm going back to the market. If you want to come back later and ask me some more questions about the story you're writing, I'll be in the market."

"Yes. I'll come by later."

I started walking back and I saw Fatoma, the maid, who lived in Arcila, walking very fast. I said, "Fatoma, what's wrong? How come you're walking fast? Where are you going?"

"I'm coming to see you because you insulted my niece."

"I didn't do anything to your niece. Please believe me. I didn't do anything to her. I was on my way to the beach and she ran into me. She asked me if I wanted to go out with her. I told her I wasn't interested. That's exactly what happened."

"No. She told me a different story."

"Well, I don't care what she told you. That's what happened."

"You told her you wanted to take her to the woods and

make love to her in broad daylight."

I apologized to her and she left.

Haskell came. He started asking me questions again. We stayed there talking for a long time, about two hours.

I said, "Why don't you forget about my story and tell me about Driss."

"I met Driss about a month ago down on the beach. I went to buy some fish, and I met him there. We started talking. He said he was scrubbing the deck of the boat and he fell and broke his leg. This happened three years ago and nobody did anything to help him. That's why I'm interested in talking to his boss." Then Haskell said, "I'm going home now. We'll see you tomorrow at the beach at two in the afternoon."

Haskell left, and a few minutes later my partner, Taib, came back. I said to myself, Oh, Allah, the thief is coming again. I hope you get me justice with him.

Taib said, "I'm here and I think I'm going to sleep here."

"Ouakha. You take care of the business now. I'm going to leave." I took 10,000 francs out of the money and I counted it in front of him. I said, "When Latif comes, tell him I took this money."

I went back home. There were a lot of people there from Tangier. I went to the kitchen and asked Meriam if she had any dinner for me. She said, "Oh, yes, here's some of that fish you bought. I fried it and it's all ready. You help yourself."

I picked up enough to eat and I had my dinner. Then I went to the beach. I stayed there. The moon was full, the sea was calm, and I listened to the waves breaking slowly, as if they were playing music, soft music. It was very peaceful. Nobody was around. That's one thing I liked very much about Arcila.

I stayed there for a while, and I walked back home and I saw the guests had started leaving. They asked me if I would accompany them out of the Medina so they wouldn't get lost.

I said, "Ouakha. Everyone follow me."

The doctor said, "Now I would like to get that watermelon you promised me."

"Ouakha, madame, it's my pleasure to serve you. We're going through the market anyway."

We walked through the Medina and it was very quiet until we got to the market. I told the doctor to help herself. She could pick out any watermelon she wanted. She picked up one watermelon and said, "This is the one I want."

"Ouakha," I said, "let me carry it for you until we get downtown to the bus station."

We walked for a while until we got to the bus station. There wasn't any bus going to Tangier at that time. It was about nine-thirty or ten o'clock in the evening.

They began to talk. They said, "What're we going to do? How're we going to get to Tangier?"

I said, "There's one solution. You could all chip in for a taxi and take a taxi from here to Tangier."

They said, "Yes. We'll do it. How much is it?"

I asked the man at the taxi stop how much he was going to charge them to take them to Tangier. He said he was willing to take them to Tangier for 6,000 francs, $12. All six of them.

I told them: "Do you understand, the man wants 6,000 francs to take you all to Tangier?"

They said, "Oh, yes, yes!"

Tangier was about 30 miles north of Arcila. The man wanted his money in advance. They gathered their money together and gave him 6,000 francs. They all got into the taxi and they drove away.

I went back to the house. I found Lalla Ann and Mr. Miles talking downstairs in the dining room. Lalla Ann asked me, "Aren't you going to go sleep in the market tonight?"

I said, "No. Tonight I'm going to sleep here."

Mr. Miles said, "It's about time you paid some attention to your job."

I said, "Usually I don't do anything here except to go shopping." I said goodnight. I went to my room and I went to sleep.

The next day I got up early. Meriam was up. She made breakfast and I had my breakfast. Then I heard Lalla Ann calling.

She said, "We're going to go for a walk today and I'd like you to come with us."

I said, "Ouakha. I'll be in the market and I'll go with you from there."

I left the house. I went back to the market and found my partner, Taib, still asleep in the middle of the watermelons. I asked him if he wanted to have breakfast.

He said, "No, thank you. I'm going home."

"Ouakha."

He left and I stayed there. The market was already getting full of people coming from all over the villages. Two country women came to me and asked me if I had seen the Nazarene lady who had spoken Moghrebi with them last Thursday. I said, "Yes. The Nazarene lady will be here a little later. If you would like to talk to her, you're welcome to stay here and wait for her."

They said, "No. We have to go and sell our things and we'll be back."

I said, "Ouakha."

My partner, Latif, came. He said, "Good morning." I said, "Good morning."

He said, "I see the market is already getting full."

"Oh, yes. It's going to be a hot and busy day. I hope we make the rest of the money we spent on the watermelons today."

The business began to pick up. We were busy—very busy. Taib came back. The three of us were so busy, we couldn't even keep up with business. Lalla Ann and Mr. Miles came. She asked me if I was ready. I said yes. I told my partners I was going to leave, and I'd be back in about two hours—whenever I could.

We started walking up the road east of Arcila. We crossed the main highway to the woods. Lalla Ann asked me if I had seen the magazine reporter.

"Yes, I saw him. I didn't talk to him. I saw him last week when he was up on the roof taking pictures of Mr. Miles. I knew he was taking pictures. I didn't know what for."

She said, "That man was looking for all the writers and painters who live in Morocco."

"I didn't know anything about him."

She asked Mr. Miles, "Why didn't you tell the man about Larbi? You know his book is coming out."

"Why don't you mind your business. This is my affair, not yours."

I told Lalla Ann, "Who is famous today, will be forgotten tomorrow. Why don't we forget about it. That man is already gone, and it won't make any difference right now. I don't even know what this magazine means. Let's change the subject to something else."

I said, "Lalla Ann, there are two campesino ladies asking about you. They said they'd be very happy if they could talk to you again. Do you remember those ladies? They invited you to the wedding. I believe they want to ask you about the wedding—if you're going."

She said, "Fine. I'll talk to those ladies when I go back to the market."

We smelled the eucalyptus trees. They smelled so powerful and so nice. Some men were watching us for most of the time as we walked. It was so strange to them, to see me with two Nazarenes. They heard the language; they began to wonder how two Nazarenes could speak Moghrebi like Mr. Miles and Lalla Ann. Two young people, a boy and a girl, came and said good morning to Mr. Miles in Moghrebi. He answered in Moghrebi. They were surprised.

They asked Lalla Ann, "Where did you learn Moghrebi?"

"I went to the mosque in Tanja to learn Moghrebi."

"Have you stayed learning Moghrebi in the mosque for a long time?"

"Oh, yes, yes. I speak Moghrebi." She said, "Goodbye, Allah ihennik," and we left.

We went back through the woods and finally we got back to the highway again. We walked downtown to the market. Mr. Miles said he was going home.

I asked Lalla Ann, "Why don't you come with me to my business? You can sit there for a while. Maybe those two ladies will come looking for you." She said yes.

I told her to walk to the business and I would go to the cafe and get her a chair. I went to the cafe and asked the qahouaji if I could borrow one of his chairs. He said, "Ouakha." I picked up the chair and I went back. I gave the chair to Lalla Ann. She sat there for a while, and then Haskell came. When Lalla Ann saw Haskell, she smiled. She was always happy when he was with her.

He said, "Ann, what are you doing here?"

She said, "I'm selling Larbi's watermelons today."

"Wouldn't you like to go on a walk?"

"No, not right now. I'm really tired. I just came from a walk." She said, "Why don't you sit down here and talk to me?"

I gave him my chair. He stayed there talking to Lalla Ann. The two country women came back and said, "Ahilan." Lalla Ann said, "Ahilan."

They said, "How are you, madame? We haven't seen you since last Thursday. Do you still want to come to the wedding we invited you to?"

She said, "I don't know if I'm going to be here next Sunday."

They asked her to tell them how she learned Moghrebi.

"I came to Morocco about 20 years ago, and I went to the mosque to learn Moghrebi."

"How beautiful! We never in our lifetimes have seen any Nazarene who speaks Moghrebi like you! We would like it very much if you could come to the wedding. There will be many women there who will ask you all sorts of different questions. If you want to come, our plan is still the same. We'll send horses to Hajra den Nhal and they'll bring you to the wedding. We hope you can come. Allah ihennik."

Haskell said, "Larbi, don't forget we have to go down to the beach to meet Driss's boss. We have to talk to him."

I said, "No. I haven't forgotten."

I told Taib to take care of business. I was going to the beach for a while. Lalla Ann said, "I'm going home." Haskell said he was going to take Ann home and he would meet me at the beach. He met me at the beach, and the fishing boats began to come in. We saw Driss in a large boat with a lot of other fishermen coming to the shore.

Everyone got out. Driss came and brought his boss to where we were standing. He introduced his boss: "This is my maallem," he said. "This is Haskell, my friend, and this is Larbi. Haskell is the man who wants to talk to you about my accident."

His boss said, "He can ask me anything he wants."

Haskell began to ask him what happened. "Why didn't Driss get medical attention for his leg?"

The maallem said, "He wasn't working at that time."

Haskell began to get very upset. He was shouting at Driss's boss. He said, "This is not right. Don't you see how he walks now? He will never be able to walk right unless he has a proper operation."

His boss said, "This was three years ago. The company doesn't even have his records anymore. He should have said something then."

Haskell asked Driss why he didn't speak for himself when this happened. Driss said there was nothing he could do.

I told Haskell, "Don't argue with this man. It will just make problems for us now. It was so long ago that people don't even want to remember it."

Haskell said, "No. This is not right. If a person gets hurt on his job, the company should take care of him."

The maallem said, "We don't have any insurance here."

Haskell said, "How come a large company like this doesn't have any insurance?"

"That's the policy of the government."

People began to gather around us. I told Haskell one more time: "Please come, let's leave this place. People here don't understand about insurance."

I apologized to Driss's boss, and I told Haskell, "Let's

go to the cafe and have some tea."

Haskell was determined to speak about the people's rights. Then I knew Haskell wasn't going to last in Morocco for very long. Haskell didn't know the laws in Morocco. The government owns the companies, and no one can file a claim against the government. I pulled Haskell's arm and told him, "Come, come, please, let's go."

The three of us walked back to the cafe and ordered three glasses of tea. Driss had just gotten paid that day, and he paid for all three of us. Haskell was still frustrated. I told him, "Why don't you forget about it?"

He said, "No! There must be a law against this."

We stayed there for a while and we finished our tea. Driss said, "See that big chunk of tuna? I'm going to take it home and fix it. I'm going to invite you to dinner. My mother would love to have you for dinner."

Haskell accepted and I said, "Now I'm going back."

I went back to the market. It was still full of people. It was the busiest day in that week. All of a sudden a holy man came and started touching the watermelons. No one said anything to him. He had a long beard and dirty feet. He didn't have any shoes on. People gave him money, and he would take the money and give it to someone else. He wanted nothing for himself. People gave him food and things, but he gave them all away. All he had was the food he ate.

He picked up one watermelon from the pile and gave it to a woman. I looked at him and I wanted to say something. My partner, Taib, winked at me. I knew he didn't want me to say anything. I didn't.

I decided to go home and have some food. When I got home, I found Mr. Miles in the house, nobody else.

I had something to eat. When I had eaten, I began

thinking about the work I did with Haskell. I said to myself, if Mr. Miles gave me half the money we made from the book, I think Haskell should give me half the money, too, when he sells his story. I think I'll go to Haskell's house and ask him.

I walked to Haskell's house and I knocked and he let me in. I asked him, "Are you going to give me half of the money you're going to make on your story?"

He said, "What do you mean? Did Miles take half of the money you made on the book?"

"Yes."

"Why does he have to take money from poor men? I'm going to go to the house and talk to him."

"Don't do that. We agreed on the whole thing."

"He should know better. He doesn't need the money as much as you do."

"What's right is right. We agreed, and I don't think you can say anything about it."

What I said to him didn't make any difference. He walked to Mr. Miles's house. He was calling, "Miles."

Mr. Miles came downstairs. Haskell said, "Why did you do that to Larbi?"

Mr. Miles said, "What are you talking about? What have I done?"

Haskell said, "You took half of Larbi's money from his book. You should be ashamed of yourself. You don't need any money."

They argued and they began shouting. I shouted that they shouldn't fight. Mr. Miles took a bottle and threw it at Haskell. The bottle hit the wall and there was glass all over the room.

Mr. Miles said, "Get out of my house! Get out! This is my house. You don't have any right to speak to me like that. I'll kill you if you don't get out of my house."

Mr. Miles began to throw plates everywhere. Then I knew he was really mad. I told Haskell, "You have to leave."

We both left the house. There were a lot of children outside the door, listening to all the noise we had been making inside.

I said to Haskell, "You see what happened? Mr. Miles is going to be mad at me for the rest of his life."

He said, "Someone had to tell him that he couldn't take your money."

I said, "We agreed."

We both left. Haskell went back home and I went down to the beach. I remembered that Lalla Ann was going to come back. I thought it would be a good idea to sweep the house before she came back. I didn't want her to know what had happened. It would make her upset.

I went back to the house and I swept the floor twice and cleaned until everything was neat again. I heard knocking on the door. I opened the door and Fatoma, the maid who lived in Arcila, wanted to get paid. I called Mr. Miles and told him: "Fatoma wants her money."

He didn't say anything to me at all. He paid her and she left. I went running after her. I told her she looked beautiful and I wanted to sleep with her.

She said, "Aren't you ashamed of yourself? You're like my son. How could you?"

"You brought me a young woman, but I didn't like her. I like you better."

"Shame! Shame! I've never met anyone like you. What's the matter with you—are you crazy? Don't you know my husband would get really mad at you?"

"I don't care about your husband. You look very beautiful to me. That's all that matters to me right now."

"Stay away from me! Stay away! You're the Devil himself."

I walked away from her and I went back to the beach. I was mad, I was lonely and I didn't know what to do. I felt shame afterward. I stayed on the beach for a while, walking back and forth.

I walked back to the market and my partner, Taib, was there alone. I told him to go home if he had anything to do and to come back so I could go for my dinner.

Taib left, and I stayed there alone. There wasn't very much business. The market was quiet for a long time. It was getting dark. My partner, Taib, came back. I told him to take care of the business. I would be back after dinner.

By the time I got back, Lalla Ann was there, and Meriam, the maid who lived in Tangier. I asked the ladies if they had any food. They said, "Yes, there's a big pot in the kitchen. Help yourself."

I didn't know if Mr. Miles had told Ann anything about our fight. I didn't say anything to her about it.

5 / The Moussem

Lalla Ann asked me, "Are you coming with us tomorrow to the moussem?"

I said, "Yes, I'd like to go if I could find transportation. The moussem only comes once a year, and I'd like to be there."

"We're going tomorrow night. If we have room, you can come with us."

"Ouakha. Now I'm going to the market, and I have to spend the night there. I'll see you in the morning, Incha Allah."

I walked back to the market. I found Latif by himself. My partner, Taib, wasn't there. I asked Latif what he thought of the business. "Are we going to make any profit or not?"

"I don't know. It's hard to say. I'm sure we will make a little money."

"What are you going to do tonight?"

"Tonight I think I'm going to come and spend the night in the market. I've lived in Arcila all my life, and I never spent a night in the market."

"Well, I could sure use some company."

"Now I'm going home; I'm going to have my dinner. I'm going to ask my wife to make us a pot of tea, and I'm going to bring it along with me when I come back."

Latif left and I stayed there alone for a while. Taib came back.

He said, "How're we doing?"

"Not so bad."

I told him that Latif was going to spend the night here with me.

He said, "That's a good idea."

He sat and we started talking for a while. Latif came back. He had a couple of blankets under his arm, a pillow, a big pot of tea and the glasses.

He said, "Salaam aleikoum to you all." He asked Taib if he wanted to go home. Taib said: "Ouakha." I told Taib I probably wouldn't be here tomorrow night; the two of them would have to work out who was going to spend the night with the watermelons.

He said, "We'll worry about tomorrow night. Incha Allah. I'll see you tomorrow morning." And he left.

It was getting late in the evening. I asked my partner, Latif, if he wanted me to help him move some watermelons so he could have enough room to sleep.

He said, "Ouakha, that's not such a bad idea."

We moved some watermelons until we had enough room to lay his blanket on the floor. We made our places. We sat right down there in the middle of all the watermelons.

Latif put his hands in his pockets and he brought out

a can of kif and a pipe. Then he poured two glasses of tea.

He smoked his first pipe. Then he smoked the second one. Then he filled the pipe and lit it and said, "Here."

I said, "I don't smoke kif, but tonight I'll smoke some."

I smoked that pipe, and I felt relaxed. I asked Latif, "What did you do before?"

He said, "I was a captain in the Spanish army before Morocco got independence. When Morocco got independence, they got rid of all of us—all the captains and the soldiers in the Spanish army. I was one of the victims. I spent twenty years of my life in the service, and they kicked me out without any pension or anything."

"Why did all this happen to you?"

"All the people who are in power in the Moroccan government, they're all from the South. The people from the South, they're the ones who are responsible for the army and the government now."

I finally understood what he was talking about. Most officials in charge of the government in Northern Morocco were from the South. They were all greedy and selfish. They even brought some officials to Tangier. They put them in the Post Office and in the Airport and in the Port, because the government never trusted the people from the North.

Latif took his wallet out and showed me pictures of himself in uniform. I said, "That's a shame, a shame. It's sad but what can we do about it? I thought independence was going to be good for all the people in Morocco, not just a few. It looks to me as though Morocco never did get any independence. We don't have the same freedom for everyone."

After a while I asked him to fill me another pipe of kif. I smoked that pipe and then he asked me, "What about you? What do you do all the time?"

I said, "Well, I work for different people wherever I can. I don't have a steady job. Most of my jobs usually last two or three months. You could say I'm more fortunate than a lot of people in Morocco."

He said he was thinking about selling his house and moving to Tangier. I told him Tangier is not the city it used to be. Then I began to feel sleepy.

I told him, "I think I'm going to go to sleep. I'll see you in the morning. Incha Allah."

Early in the morning I went to the beach around the corner. I stayed there for a while. When I came back, I found my partner already awake. I told him I was going home. I would be back as soon as possible so he could go home.

I went home. Lalla Ann was already up. I said, "Good morning, Lalla Ann." She said, "Good morning. How did you sleep?"

"Fine."

I asked her when they were going to go to the moussem. She said they'd probably leave about six or seven o'clock in the afternoon.

"There are some people coming from Tangier. They're going to pick us up and take us to the moussem."

I told Lalla Ann, "When you're ready to leave this afternoon, if you have room, please come by the market. And take some watermelons with you. It's going to be hot during the day."

I went back to the market. I found my partner, Taib, there already. I told my two partners I was going to the moussem, so they would have to arrange something for tonight.

Latif left. Taib and I stayed there. People began to come to the market. Then Fatoma's husband came and said, "Salaam aleikoum. I want to talk to you."

I said, "Ouakha. Let's walk."

"Aren't you ashamed of yourself? Trying to make love to my wife. She's as old as your mother."

"I'm sorry, my good man. I don't know what came over me."

"Shame. Shame. I'm going to go and tell your boss about it."

He left and went to the house. I walked back to the business and I saw Lalla Ann and Haskell coming.

Haskell said, "Buenos dias."

I said, "Buenos dias."

He said, "We're going to go to the beach. Do you want to come with us?"

"Ouakha." I told Taib I would be back in a little while.

We walked toward the beach. Near the beach we found two women arguing.

One woman was the owner of a house and the other woman was renting from her. She didn't have enough money to pay the rent.

Lalla Ann asked the women why they were fighting. The woman who owned the house told Lalla Ann that the other woman was living in her house, and she hadn't paid rent for six months.

The woman who hadn't paid the rent started crying. She said, "I don't have any money and I don't have any job. I don't know how I'm going to pay the rent to this lady. My husband is in the army, but he hasn't sent me any money for so long."

I looked at the woman who was crying and I felt sad, very sad.

Lalla Ann asked the woman who was the owner how much money the other woman owed her.

She said she owed her 6,000 francs for six months.

Lalla Ann said, "Ouakha. I'll tell you what I'm going to do. I'll pay you for the six months, and I'll pay you for six extra months in case her husband doesn't send her any money."

The owner agreed and asked Lalla Ann for the money.

Lalla Ann said she didn't have the money with her. If the woman would come to her house she would pay her.

The owner said, "I don't know you. I've never seen you before. How can I trust you?"

"If you don't trust me, come with me now. Let's go to my house and I'll pay you."

All five of us walked back to the house, and Lalla Ann went to her room and brought back 12,000 francs, $24.00, to pay the owner. The owner left and the other woman came to the door. She had followed us, not very close. I opened the door and the woman said, "I want to talk to that Nazarene lady."

Lalla Ann came to her and shook her hand. The woman started kissing her hand.

Lalla Ann said, "La. La. No. No."

The women kept trying to kiss Lalla Ann's hand and Lalla Ann took her hand away.

She said, "No. No. You don't have to say anything to me."

The woman told her she had never met a Nazarene like her in her life. She said she had never met any Nazarene lady who spoke Moghrebi.

I knew Lalla Ann was always doing good for people. I wished there were more people like Lalla Ann in the world.

Lalla Ann went back to her room and Mr. Miles came downstairs and he said, "What happened between you and the husband of Fatoma?"

"Nothing."

"You wanted to make love to his wife."

"Yes, I did. So what?"

"I'm just asking you. It's not my business. I just don't want any trouble with the maid."

The whole morning was turning sour again. I closed the door and left the house. I said, Oh, Allah, please forgive me.

When I walked back to the market, I told my partners, "I'm going to be away for maybe two or three days. You take care of the business, and I want Latif to keep the money until I come back."

Latif said, "Ouakha. Don't worry about it. Enjoy yourself. We'll take care of everything."

I counted the money and there were 11,000 francs. I took that money and I got some more at home. I took 30,000 francs and paid Mr. Miles what he had lent me earlier. I asked Mr. Miles if he thought they had enough space for me to ride with them to the moussem.

He said, "I don't know. I know there are a lot of people coming this afternoon."

I said, "Ouakha. I'll just have to wait until this afternoon when the people come to get you and Ann and Meriam. I'd like to go if there's room."

In a little while I heard a car horn blowing. The people left their cars by the palace and they walked to Mr. Miles's house. I opened the door and they asked, "Where are Miles and Ann?"

I said, "Come on in."

They came in. There were eight people. There were three girls and five men. They spoke French and English.

Lalla Ann and Mr. Miles came down and they began to talk and make plans about how to get to the moussem. They asked Lalla Ann if she knew where the moussem was.

She said yes. They said, "We've got everything. We've got food, we've got drinks. We've got everything we need."

Meriam packed up all the food. She had two baskets full of food already cooked and ready to go. Meriam said, "Take these baskets to the car where the man is waiting."

I took the two baskets to the car. The man asked me how long I had known Mr. Miles and Lalla Ann. I said I had known them for a long time. He asked me if I liked working for them. I said yes.

He asked me if I was going to go to the moussem with them. I said, "Yes, but I don't know if there's going to be space for me."

He said, "We probably have enough space for you."

The people followed. They got in and there was still enough space for two more. One of the men said, "We're ready to go. We have to pick up two more people."

I said, "Do you have space for me?"

He said, "No, it doesn't look like it."

"Why don't I ride in the trunk?"

"Oh, no! It's very dangerous."

"What's so dangerous about it?"

He insisted that he wouldn't take me with him.

"Ouakha. I'm going regardless of how I get there. I'm going to go."

They started the cars and left. I walked back home and I picked up some food and one blanket. And I said, "Moussem here I come."

I started walking. It was about seven o'clock. The sun was just beginning to cool off. I got downtown to the bus station and I went to the counter. I asked if there were any buses leaving for Tangier.

The man said, "No. There are no buses until eleven o'clock at night. And probably by that time there will be no room left because there are already a lot of people here with tickets."

I said to myself, I don't think I'm going to get a ride either way—paying for it or not. If I want to get there, I'd better start walking.

I started walking along the beach. I walked and walked to a small village four miles out of Arcila where they made salt. A shepherd hollered at me, "Hey, what are you doing walking around here? I've never seen you before."

I said, "Oh, yes, I'm not from here. I'm from Arcila."

"Where are you going, all by yourself?"

"I'm going to the moussem."

"The moussem is very far from here. Do you think you can walk all that distance by yourself?"

"Oh, yes. This is very easy."

"Good luck." And I kept walking by the shore.

It was getting dark. I decided to walk on the highway so I could see the light. I kept walking all night long. By morning I was on the other side of the new highway. I began to hear birds singing in the wheat fields. It was about six o'clock, and I was getting very tired. The sun was coming out. I was only halfway to the moussem.

I decided to get under a tree. There were a lot of eucalyptus trees by the highway. I sat down under one big tree and my feet felt a lot better. I sat down under that shady tree and I said to myself that I wasn't going to move unless someone picked me up.

There I was sitting and my hand was held up hitchhiking. About two hours went by and I didn't get a ride. The sun by then was really hot. You could fry an egg on a stone.

I stayed there. I saw this old Volkswagen coming very slowly. It stopped in front of me.

I said, "Buenos dias." A man said, "Buenos dias." He said it with an English accent. He was an American. He asked me where I was going.

I said, "I'm going to the moussem." He said, "What is a moussem?"

"A moussem is a festival which comes once a year. This one always comes in summer. People come from all over the country to take part in it."

"What do all the people do?"

"There are musicians, people selling food and jewelry. It's like a market, but it's more like a festival."

"Anybody could go there?"

"Yes, anybody could go there."

"Even Nazarenes?"

"Yes. Even Nazarenes."

"Come. I'll give you a ride to the entrance of the airport."

"Ouakha." I said to myself, Once I get there it will be easy to get a ride because everyone will be going in the direction of the moussem.

I got into the car and we drove away. He asked me my name. I said my name was Larbi. He said his name was Paul Manheim.

I said, "What are you doing in Morocco?"

"I'm visiting. I'm also trying to arrange for some musicians to come to Tangier." He asked me where I was coming from. I said I came from Arcila.

"How could you walk that far?"

"I started yesterday afternoon."

We kept driving. He made a left turn on the way to the Tangier airport. We got to the entrance and he said, "I've got to let you off here. I'm going to Tangier. I'm not going to go to the moussem."

He left and I stayed there hitchhiking toward the airport. There were lots of cars going to the moussem. I saw a friend of mine named Farid. He was driving a jeep. He stopped right where I was standing.

There were four of them in the jeep: his mother and his two sisters. He asked me what I was doing there. I said I was trying to get a ride to the moussem. Would he take me?

He said, "No, this is a private car. It's for our family only."

I looked at him and I felt so ashamed. I didn't know what to make of it. I was the one who had got him the job as a chauffeur.

He drove away and I stood there. A taxi with five people in it stopped. The driver asked me where I was going. I said, "I'm going to the moussem. Can you take me?"

He said, "Ouakha. I'll take you for 500 francs."

I paid him and we drove all the way to the airport. From the airport to the beach it was a dirt road. It was so dusty you couldn't see very far ahead. Finally, we got to the moussem.

I was very hungry. I went looking for food right away. I found a man who made pinchitos. I asked him to give me three skewers and put them in a half a loaf of French bread. I ordered a glass of tea and I sat. There were lines and lines of cars coming.

I finished my food and I started walking around to see if I could find some people I knew. I found Mustafa's family there. Mustafa's sister said, "Oh, Larbi, what are you doing here? Why didn't you come with us?"

I said, "I'm sorry. I didn't come from Tangier. I came from Arcila."

She asked me, "Didn't you bring your family with you?"

"No. I came alone." I asked her, "Where are all of you staying?"

"See that black tent up there? That's our tent."

"Can I sleep there? I'm very tired. I didn't sleep all night last night."

She took me to the tent. Her mother said, "Oh, Larbi, what are you doing here?"

"I came to the moussem."

"Aren't you hungry?"

"No, I just had my breakfast. I'm really tired. I'd like to sleep."

"See how much room we have here? Make yourself at home. Sleep anywhere you want."

She gave me a big blanket and a pillow and said, "Here. Make yourself at home. Wake up when you've had enough sleep."

I knew that was what I needed. There were a lot of children in the tent. They didn't even bother me. I fell asleep. I slept five or six hours. It was late in the afternoon when I woke up.

I washed my face and I walked out of the tent. I went straight to the tomb of Si Abdeslam. I went in and took a donation out of my pocket and gave it to the man who was saying prayers for the people who had come to the moussem. There were other men there saying prayers, too.

The man began to say a prayer for me. I said, "I don't really need any prayer, but I do need some good luck."

They kept saying the prayer, and I left. I joined the hundreds of people outside. Everybody was happy and excited. There were lots of musicians and people who cast spells against sickness and bad luck. There were cafe stands that were very crowded. I saw Mustafa in a big tent. He had a huge box filled with ice and Coca Cola. He said,

"Larbi, where have you been? I've been looking for you all over the place. What happened to you? I wanted to make you a partner in the business here."

"I have a job working in Arcila."

"When did you come to the moussem?"

"I came this morning."

"Have you seen our tent?"

"Yes, I slept there almost all day."

"Good. You must be rested. Why don't you stay here? I'm going to Tangier and get some ice. Otherwise the Coca Cola won't be any good."

"Listen, I didn't come here to work. I came to enjoy myself."

"What kind of friend are you? I can't depend on you for anything. Stay here for a while. My brother, Abdeslam, will relieve you. Don't worry, you won't have to stay here all night."

I asked him, "How much are you selling the Coca Cola for?"

"Fifty francs each."

"Ouakha."

He drove back to Tangier and I stayed with the business.

The business was very good. The sun began to go down and the day was getting cool. I stayed there about two hours and Abdeslam came over.

He said, "Larbi, where did you come from?"

"I've been here all day long. I just didn't see you."

"What happened to my brother?"

"Your brother went to Tangier to buy some ice."

"How is the business?"

"Not so bad."

A few minutes later I saw Mr. Miles coming with a lot

of Europeans, French, Spanish and English. He looked at me and said, "When did you get here?"

"This morning."

"Are you working here now?"

"No, I'm just helping my friend."

He introduced me to some of the people. I shook their hands. I asked them if they wanted any Coca Cola. They said, "No. No Coca Cola."

Mr. Miles said, "Well, I'll see you later. When are you going back to Arcila? Nobody's in the house."

"Don't worry about the house. Nobody's going to take anything. In two or three days I'll be back there."

He took all those people with him, and they began going around to see the festival. He was like a guide for all those people. They had never seen a Moroccan festival. He was the translator, too. They kept laughing as they walked away.

A little bit later Mustafa came back with ice. He asked me to go with him to the car to bring the ice over. We brought all the ice in and a few minutes later I saw Lalla Ann with her maid, Habiba, and the cab driver, Boulaich. They were all laughing and having a good time. They saw me talking to Mustafa.

Lalla Ann said, "Larbi, we left you in Arcila, and you're here now. How did you get here?"

"If I told you what happened, you wouldn't believe me."

She started laughing. I told her how I got to the moussem.

Lalla Ann said she was very tired of walking and she wanted to rest for a while. I told her if she wanted to rest, I could talk to my friend Mustafa's mother, and she would probably let Lalla Ann rest in their tent.

She said, "Do I know the people?"

I said, "Mustafa is right here. You know Mustafa."

She said, "No, I've seen him before, but I don't know him."

I said, "He is the man who owns the cafe down by Merkala."

Mustafa said, "Ahilan," and shook her hand.

I asked Mustafa if his mother would let Lalla Ann rest for a while. He said, "Oh, yes. My mother wouldn't object to Ann resting in her tent. Why don't you take Ann with you, and go talk to my mother?"

Lalla Ann and I walked across the road until we got to Mustafa's tent. I asked his mother if she would let my friend Lalla Ann rest for a while.

She said, "Oh, yes, Aoulidi. Come on in. Come on in."

Lalla Ann began to talk to Mustafa's mother in Moghrebi. They became friendlier. It was very easy for Mustafa's mother to understand Lalla Ann. She asked her to sit down.

I said, "Now you'll be able to talk together," and I left the ladies in the tent.

I went back to the Coca Cola stand and I stayed there talking to Mustafa. Boulaich came back and asked me if we were going to put in a little money each so we could buy enough food to cook dinner.

Mustafa said, "No. We brought plenty of food. Anytime you get hungry, Larbi, just go to the tent."

Boulaich said, "I'm hungry now."

I said, "Why don't you go buy some pinchitos and bring them back? Then you can sit down and have something to eat."

He said, "That's a good idea." He went and bought some pinchitos and a half loaf of bread. He sat down and asked me how long I had known Ann, and where I had met her.

I said, "I met Lalla Ann a long time ago at Merkala, at Mustafa's cafe. I was so surprised when I met her for the first time. She spoke Moghrebi."

I asked him, "How did you meet Lalla Ann?"

"I met Ann a long time ago on the ferry boat from Spain. Since then she always recommends me to tourists who need a driver. She gets me many trips driving people all over Morocco."

We kept talking, Boulaich and I. There were all kinds of different sounds of music around us. Each group was making its own music. There was a group of Gnaoua pounding drums, so loud they shook the ground. There were Jilala holding their drums up in the air, and there were some Aissaoua beating light drums while their cobras danced. When the music stopped, the ocean sounded far away, but it wasn't far. It was only a hundred yards from the moussem. Then the ocean began to make its own music.

We stayed there talking. Later Lalla Ann came over. I asked her if she had had enough rest.

She said, "Yes. Now I feel better. I'm going to stay here until early morning and then I'll go home."

Boulaich took Lalla Ann's hand as they walked, watching the festivities. Mustafa's sister came over to tell us that dinner was ready.

She said, "Larbi, where did you meet that Nazarene lady who speaks Moghrebi?"

I said, "I met her in your brother's cafe down at Merkala."

She said, "Where did she learn Moghrebi?"

I said, "She's been here for a long time."

She said, "I never met any Nazarene lady who speaks Moghrebi perfectly the way she does. I hope she'll come back and see us sometime."

Mustafa said, "Larbi, if you're hungry now, why don't you go to my mother's tent?"

I said, "No, thank you, I'm not hungry. I'm going to the beach."

I walked through the festival. I got to the beach. By the time I got to the water, I no longer heard the music the people were making. The waves were breaking and a gentle wind was blowing. The sky was full of stars. The moon was halfway full. I liked the gentle waves. I stayed there listening for a while.

Then I went back to the festivities and I watched all the people dancing and the drummers beating their drums. It was getting late, about two-thirty or three in the morning. People began to leave. The ones with cars went to the city. The ones who stayed went to their tents.

I went to Mustafa's tent and almost everybody was asleep except Mustafa's brother, who was still up.

I asked him, "Are you going to sleep here, or are you going to the Coca Cola stand?"

He said he was going to go and relieve his brother so Mustafa would have enough sleep. He asked me, "What about you?"

"I'm very tired and I want to go to sleep."

He gave me a woolen blanket and he said, "Find yourself a space and sleep anywhere you want." I did.

When I got up later in the morning, the sun was already high in the sky and it was getting very hot. I decided to go to Tangier to see my wife. I took a taxi with some other people and we drove the six or seven miles to Tangier. The taxi took us all to the Zoco. From there I took a bus home.

When I opened the door, I found a strange man in my house with my wife. I asked him, "What are you doing in my house?"

He said, "I'm your neighbor. I'm a guard across the street."

I asked my wife, "Why did you let him in?"

She said, "I was just talking to him."

I didn't even know what to say anymore — to my wife, to the strange man I found in my house. I slammed the door and I left. I went straight down to the Avenida de España. I bought a ticket for Arcila and got on the bus.

We drove about an hour or so, until we got to Arcila. I got off the bus and went straight to the watermelons. I found my partner, Taib, there. I asked him, "How was the business?"

He said, "Very good."

I noticed the pile of watermelons was getting smaller and smaller.

I told my partner, Taib, "I'm going to go and check on the house."

I walked home and I found Fatoma there cleaning the house. She asked me, "What happened to all the people? What happened to Mr. Miles and Lalla Ann?"

I told her they would be back the day after tomorrow.

She said, "Who's going to pay me?"

I said, "When Mr. Miles comes back, he's going to pay you. You don't have to worry about it."

I told Fatoma if she needed anything she could come to the market.

I left the house and I went back to the market. I told my partner to go home and come back that evening. I stayed in the market all the rest of the day. Latif came and brought a big plate of food. He said, "Are you hungry? This is my dinner. Let's eat."

We had our dinner. He said, "Well, it's my turn tonight. I'm going to stay here in the market to watch the watermelons."

I said, "Ouakha, if you want to stay here tonight it's all right with me." I went back home and I stayed there the evening.

Two days later, Mr. Miles came back. Mr. Miles didn't say anything to me. I supposed he was still angry. I didn't talk to him.

We stayed in Arcila, today and tomorrow, until one night the water began to leak down into my room. And the water smelled bad. I went upstairs and I asked Mr. Miles if there was anything wrong with the plumbing in the bathroom.

He said, "Yes. The toilet is clogged up and I don't know what's wrong with it."

I said, "Let me look."

I saw that the toilet was full of water, the drain wasn't working. I asked Mr. Miles how long the toilet had been clogged.

He said he didn't know. When he came home, it was already clogged up.

I tried to unplug the toilet, but it didn't work.

Mr. Miles said, "Somebody stole my gold ring. Or I might have dropped it in the toilet. Why don't you put your hand in the toilet and see if my ring is there?"

I knew he was still mad. I said to myself, "I think this man wants satisfaction. I'm going to give it to him."

I rolled up my shirt sleeves and I stuck my hand into the toilet. I squeezed with my hand all that water and shit, but I didn't find any ring in there. All I found was a roll of paper clogging the drain. I pulled out that roll of paper and I looked at Mr. Miles and he looked very happy.

I said, "Well, this is what I found in the toilet; as you can see, no ring." I took the paper and put it in the garbage can, and I washed my hands.

He said, "If you didn't find my ring there, the maid you brought to work for me probably stole it."

"I didn't bring that maid to work for you. The man who's in charge of the house, who gave you the key, he's the one who found her."

"Well, you're responsible. You're supposed to watch over the house."

"I'm not responsible for what the maid does. I make sure nobody breaks into the house."

"Why don't you go to Fatoma's house and ask her if she stole my ring?"

"I don't know where Fatoma lives. She'll be here in the morning. You ask her yourself."

"What kind of a houseboy are you, not to watch over people's things?"

The next day Fatoma came in the morning. I told her, "We have something missing from the house and I'd like to know if you stole anything."

The poor woman began to cry. I felt sad. I had accused her of something, and I didn't even know if she had done it.

I said, "Please don't cry. Forgive me. I'm just telling you what Mr. Miles told me. Someone stole his ring and I don't know who. Mr. Miles is going to ask you about the ring. If you didn't take it, all you have to do is tell him."

"Aren't you ashamed of yourself, accusing me of stealing!"

"I don't know anything about it. I'm being accused myself. I'm going out. Mr. Miles will probably talk to you later."

I went to my room and I picked up all my clothes and I went down to the beach and washed everything in salt water to get rid of the smell. I rinsed everything in the fresh water fountain in the Medina. I took the wash to the roof and hung it up to dry. I left it there and I decided that night I would stay in the hammam, the steambath, because I didn't have any clothes.

I went to the hammam and I paid 100 francs. I took my clothes off and I went in to the steamroom. I stayed there for a long, long time, until about four o'clock in the morning. I heard a man calling for the prayer, and I knew it was morning. I left the steamroom and I went to the room with the mats. I stayed there cooling myself off for a while. I got dressed and I left the hammam. I went to the beach. I stayed there until daylight.

I left the beach and went back to the market and told my partner, Latif, that I would stay there if he wanted to go home.

He left and I stayed there. The stores began to open and the cafe opened.

I went to the cafe. I asked the qahouaji to make me a glass of *café con leche.* I went to the pastry man and I asked him to give me two sfinjes. He tied them on a string and gave them to me.

I went back to the watermelons. The qahouaji brought me the glass. I paid him and he left. I could see campesinos coming with their donkeys and horses loaded with food.

6 / The Wedding

I saw the two country women who had been talking to Lalla Ann. They came straight to my stall.

They said, "Good morning."

I said, "Good morning, ladies."

They asked, "Is that Nazarene lady going to be here today? We're asking you about her because tomorrow we're having the wedding. We came to find out if she is coming, so we can have horses ready to meet her."

I said, "Yes, the lady will be here tomorrow afternoon. I don't know what time. I'll ask her if she still wants to come to the wedding. If she does, I'll bring her with me."

One of the country women said, "Ouakha, she will come. She said she wanted to come to the wedding. She gave us her word."

I said, "Ouakha, if she comes, we'll both come to the wedding, if I'm invited."

"Ouakha, ouakha. If you're a friend of the lady, you're welcome to come."

"Ouakha, tell me where to meet the people who will pick us up with the horses."

"You take a bus from Arcila. The bus leaves tomorrow afternoon at five o'clock. There's a one hour ride. I'll have my shepherd meet you in Hajra den Nhal."

"Ouakha. We'll see you tomorrow evening. Incha Allah. If the lady comes, she'll be with me. If she doesn't come, I'll be alone."

They said, "That's it, it's settled."

I said, "Ouakha."

The ladies walked down a couple of yards and set up their business. They set out baskets of carrots, tomatoes, and onions. They had peanuts, walnuts and almonds.

My two partners came back. We stayed all day long. Late in the afternoon Haskell came.

He asked me, "How was the moussem?"

"It was very good."

"What is your plan, after you finish working for Miles in Arcila?"

"I don't know. I don't really have a plan. I just have to go back to Tangier and see if I can find another job."

He asked me, "Do you know if Ann is coming tomorrow?"

"I don't know. I hope she does. She's invited to the wedding."

"Who invited her?"

"Some country women. They like her very much. They can talk to her. She makes them feel very good. She understands the language."

Haskell said, "Okay, I'm going down to the beach to see if Driss's boat came in."

He left.

I told my partner, Taib, "I'm hungry. I've got to go and get something to eat."

"Why don't you wait a minute. My son is bringing food. I told him to bring enough for two or three people. We could eat together."

"I'm going to ask for some glasses of tea."

I took my empty glass back to the cafe, and I asked the qahouaji to make three glasses of tea. A little bit later the qahouaji brought the tea, and Taib's son brought the food. He brought some pastry, too.

I said to the young man, "Why don't you take a watermelon home? You might be thirsty."

Taib said, "Well, you want to eat now?"

"Ouakha, let's eat now while the food is warm."

Latif said he was going home. His wife was waiting for him.

We started eating our food. I told Taib when I finished I was going home and get my clothes from the roof.

He said, "Did you do your wash?"

"Yes, I had to wash some things."

"Ouakha. I'm going to sleep here tonight and you can go home."

We finished eating. I told my partner I would see him in the morning. I went home.

I went up to the roof and found my wash dry. I sniffed; it didn't smell. I picked up everything and I went downstairs to my room. I made my bed and I went to sleep.

In the morning I got up and I washed and I had my breakfast. On the way out I saw Mr. Miles and I said, "Good morning," and he didn't answer back.

I said, "Tonight I'm going to a wedding if it's all right with you."

"Where is the wedding going to be?"

"It's going to be up in the mountains." I asked him what time Ann was coming.

He said, "She will be here about one o'clock."

"Are you going to go and meet her, or do you want me to go and meet her?"

"No, I'm going to meet her."

I said, "Ouakha," and I left.

I went back to the market, and I found my partner, Latif, already there. I told my partner, Taib, that if he wanted to go home, he could. Taib left and we stayed there. There wasn't very much business all that day. About one-thirty in the afternoon I saw Lalla Ann and Mr. Miles walking toward me.

I said, "Ahilan," to Lalla Ann. I asked her if she remembered the wedding.

She said, "Yes, that's why I came. I want to go to that wedding. I've never been to a country wedding. This will be very interesting."

I said, "Ouakha. We'll go this afternoon at five o'clock. We take a bus from here and go to the village. When we arrive, there will be horses waiting for us."

Mr. Miles said, "Why wasn't I told about this?"

I said, "You weren't invited."

He said, "Ann shouldn't go to the country. She's not feeling very well."

I said, "Why don't you ask Lalla Ann and see what she says."

Lalla Ann said, "No, I want to go. I promised the ladies I was going. I even brought a gift for the bride."

Mr. Miles said, "Fine. You be careful. Be careful nothing happens to Ann."

"Don't worry, nothing's going to happen to her. She

will have a good time."

He said, "How are you going to come back?"

"We're not coming back the same night. We're coming back in the morning, Incha Allah."

"Ann can't stay out the whole night. Sometimes she's not well."

He asked Ann, "Why don't I come with you?"

She said, "Because you weren't invited."

He said, "Okay. We're going home now."

I told Lalla Ann, "I'll come at four to pick you up. Then we'll walk to the bus station."

I told my partner, Latif, "I can't stay here tonight. I'm going to the wedding. You'll have to stay."

I stayed in the market until four o'clock. I told Latif I was going to leave. He said, "Ouakha."

I went to the house. I asked Lalla Ann if she was ready to leave.

She said, "Ouakha, I'm ready."

The maid, Habiba, said, "I'd better go with you in case Ann doesn't feel well."

I said, "I don't know; you weren't invited. The ladies in the village might feel strange."

Lalla Ann said, "Don't worry, nothing's going to happen to me. Everybody's worried about me, but nothing's going to happen. I'm just going to go to the wedding. Pick up that basket and let's go."

I picked up the basket and we started on our way to the bus station. We walked through the Medina until we got to the station. I went to the bus and there was a man there selling tickets. I said I wanted two tickets for Hajra den Nhal. I paid the man and I said to Lalla Ann, "Good. Get in." We both sat down in our seats and we waited for a while. Finally the bus was loaded with people and the driver said, "Now, everyone sit in your seat. We're on our way to Hajra den Nhal."

The bus took off and we went up to the mountains on a winding road until we got to Hajra den Nhal. We got off the bus. We saw a man with three horses standing where the bus stopped.

I said, "Ahilan. Are you the shepherd of the lady called Lalaicha?"

He said, "Are you the man and the Nazarene lady I'm supposed to take to Lalaicha's wedding?"

I said, "Yes."

He asked me, "Does the lady know how to ride horses?"

"I don't think so."

"Ouakha, let's help the lady get on the horse. Then you get on your horse and we'll be on our way."

We helped Lalla Ann on the horse. The shepherd said, "I'll show you an easy way. Put both legs by the horse's neck, then sit on the saddle sideways." And that's exactly what she did.

I mounted my horse and he mounted his and we started on our way. We rode halfway to the village and there was a big house and a big orchard. There were trees everywhere full of fruit and a lot of children running around. I said to myself, "That's got to be the place where the wedding is." Finally we got to the house. I got off my horse and helped Lalla Ann get down from hers.

I said, "How was the ride?"

She said, "Fine. I didn't think I'd be able to ride a horse. It was very comfortable."

The shepherd took the horses away. Lalaicha, who invited us, came out. She came to me, "Ahilan. Welcome." She went to Lalla Ann and gave her a big hug and said, "Ahilan. I'm glad you could come."

The lady told a boy to take me where the men were sitting.

She said to Lalla Ann, "Come in. Come in. I want you to meet some of our guests. This is the best thing that could have happened. We've never had a Nazarene lady here before and you speak Moghrebi like we do."

Lalla Ann went with her and I went where the men were sitting. It was a big room with large cushions all over the floor and red, yellow and blue woolen rugs. One man was pouring tea and he said, "Sit down. Do you want a glass of tea?"

I said, "Ouakha."

I sat down and drank my tea. There was a group of musicians there playing music, drinking tea and smoking kif. The room was crowded and smoky and very noisy. More people came in and there was not enough room inside. The father of the bride decided to make room outside for all the guests to sit down. He went to his neighbor and borrowed all the cushions they had and some mats and rugs to put on the floor. They made enough space for everyone who came. The musicians decided it was too hot inside, and they wanted to sit outside. It was summer and the moon was full. I felt better myself when I went out and sat down and breathed some fresh air. One musician announced that they would begin receiving the gifts for the groom. They put out a big round taifor about three feet high and each time they received a gift they announced it: This gift is from Mr. So and So, 3,000 francs; this gift is from Mr. So and So, 10,000 francs. They announced every gift they received, and the taifor was piled high with money. I heard the women announcing their gifts in the other room. The musicians were calling, "Come on, give some more, give some more." Everyone had to give. I gave them my gift of 3,000 francs.

They picked up the tablecloth full of all the money and they gave it to the father of the bride. The dinner was announced. They began to bring large dishes with couscous and lamb and zucchini and carrots. We made small circles, about ten people to a circle. They put a dish in the center. We all started eating with our fingers. We ate and ate, there was so much food. They said, "Come on. Everyone must eat some more." But the people were full and couldn't eat any more.

They picked up all the dishes and we sat back the way we were. They brought out the tea and pastry. Everyone had one pastry and a glass of tea. They gave us each a small loaf of bread baked with honey and almonds to take with us.

The musicians began to play songs for the people who requested them. You had to pay 500 francs for each song you asked for. They played music for a long time until the musicians were tired. It was about three o'clock in the morning. One musician talked to the father of the bride. He said it was time to take the bride outside to walk around the house. The father of the bride went to his wife and told her the musicians were ready. It was time to get all the people outside for the walk around the house.

All the women began to walk and at the center of all the women the bride walked. The musicians followed them playing songs for the bride. They walked in a circle around the house. All the women were dressed in white. Lalla Ann had a white blouse on. She was wearing a brown skirt. I walked to Lalla Ann and asked her how she liked the wedding.

She said, "This is a wonderful thing. I'm so glad I came."

The father of the bride came over to me and said, "Aren't you ashamed—talking to the ladies!"

I said, "No, my good man, this is a friend of mine."

He said, "Aren't you ashamed of yourself? It's not customary to talk to the women at the wedding."

I apologized to him and I went back where the men were sitting. I sat with them.

The women kept walking in a circle. The moon was full. The night was made for the wedding. The moon was so close to the women as they walked in a circle, it was like a magic light shining on all of them. They went around the house twice. Then they went back to their room.

The musicians left. The people began to leave, except for the guests who were going to sleep there. It was getting very, very late—it was early morning. I was very tired and I fell asleep on a mat until morning. I heard knocking on the door. The father of the bride said it was time for breakfast. They brought us pancakes with honey and tea. We ate and I left the room. I found Lalla Ann outside with Lalaicha, the mother of the bride.

I said, "Good morning." I asked her, "What do you think of my friend?"

"Oh, this is the best thing that ever happened in our village."

All the women talked to Lalla Ann at once. She made them laugh and laugh. She answered all their questions. They were surprised to see that such a lady existed.

Lalla Ann asked me if I was ready to go. I said: "Ouakha." Lalaicha called the shepherd and told him to get the horses ready. He went to the barn and saddled the horses and brought them to us. Lalla Ann hugged the lady and kissed her and said, "Thank you very much for inviting me. Allah ihennik. If you are ever in Arcila, you must come to see me. My house is by the sea cliff. Anyone can show you the house."

I helped Lalla Ann up on her horse. I got on mine. The shepherd got on his. We started back to the bus stop.

It's customary for the bride to go to her husband's house the night after the wedding party. I asked the shepherd when she would go. He said she would be taken to her husband's house this evening. He lived about a mile away, further up in the mountains.

We got to the bus stop. I helped Lalla Ann off her horse and she thanked the shepherd. He went back to the house. Lalla Ann and I began to talk in Moghrebi. Some women began to laugh. It was not possible to hear a Nazarene lady speak in Moghrebi. Lalla Ann laughed and said, "Yes, I speak Moghrebi."

The women became interested and came close and began to talk to her. I just stood there and watched. The ladies wanted to outsmart Lalla Ann with the language, but she knew it so well she didn't have any problems communicating with them. They thought she was a missionary. She said, "No, no, no, I'm not a missionary!"

Finally the bus for Arcila arrived. The bus was very crowded. A man stood up and told Lalla Ann to sit down. She sat and I stood up. The bus took off. We rode about an hour until we reached Arcila.

Lalla Ann said, "I'm very tired. I'm going to take a taxi home." She took a taxi and I went to the watermelons. I found my partner, Taib, there.

I said, "How are you?"

He said, "Fine. Where did you go?"

"I went to the wedding."

"Did you eat any hashish?"

"No, but I smoked some kif." Then I asked him what he thought of selling the watermelons cheaper so we could get rid of them sooner.

"How much cheaper should we sell them?"

"I don't know—what do you think?"

"What about 12 francs?"

"Ten francs would be better. That way we could sell them a lot faster."

We agreed to sell them for 10 francs a kilo. Soon we had many people wanting to buy the watermelons. Late in the afternoon I told my partner, Taib, I was going home. I would be back later in the evening to spend the night.

I left and I went back to the house. I asked Habiba if she had any food.

She said, "Yes, there are some fried fish there and some fried potatoes. You can help yourself." She said, "Larbi, I'm mad at you for not taking me with you to the wedding. Ann told me what a good time she had. I bet you anything if I'd gone with you, I would have known some of those ladies. I would have gotten along fine with them."

I said, "I'm sorry. The wedding wasn't mine. I couldn't invite you."

She was really mad. Mr. Miles came downstairs and I saw he was wearing a ring on his finger.

I said, "Is that the ring you said was stolen?"

He said, "Yes, I found it in my room."

"The ring was never stolen, was it?"

"It was lost and I couldn't find it, so I thought somebody stole it."

"Are you going to tell Fatoma about the ring?"

"Yes, I'll tell Fatoma. Don't worry."

I had something to eat. I thanked Habiba for the food and I left the house.

I was angry about the ring I had accused the maid of stealing. I went back to the market and told my two partners if they wanted to go home it was all right, and they left and I stayed in the market. A little bit later the dirty holy man came back to the business. He asked me if he could have some money.

I said, "Ouakha. Help yourself."

I gave him the money basket and he took 100 francs. He took a watermelon and gave it to another man. I didn't say anything. Then he took his hand and slapped me hard in the face. I wondered why he did that. I said to myself, What's wrong with this man? He's a holy man—why does he do such crazy things?

I was going to say something to him when two men came up and said, "Don't you say anything! Don't you know he's the holiest man in Arcila! You are lucky that he came to you and took some of your money and slapped you. You are very fortunate."

I said, "So that's what he means by slapping me, to give me good luck."

They said, "Yes."

The holy man went away and the men began to laugh. I knew something was wrong, but I didn't know what it was. I said to myself, This is my luck, as usual. Wherever I go, whatever I do, something happens to me. I guess I'm one of the fortunate people.

I spent the night at the market. The next day I began to think about the two men who had taken my jewelry to sell in Spain. I hadn't heard from them and I wondered if I ever would. A little bit later my partners came. Then Fatoma and her husband came to the market. They said, "Salaam aleikoum."

Her husband said, "Aren't you ashamed of yourself, accusing my wife of stealing. My wife is the most honest person you could ever have working for you."

I apologized to him and told him that the man I worked

for had found his ring. Fatoma and her husband left and went to the house. A little bit later Lalla Ann and Haskell came by.

i asked them where they were going. Haskell said he was taking Ann for a walk down the beach.

Haskell said, "Next time you go to one of those weddings, I want to go. Ann's been telling me what a good time she had."

I said, "I don't know if we'll be invited to another wedding. It happened just by luck. It was Lalla Ann the country women liked. That's why they invited us."

Haskell asked me if I wanted to go to the beach with them.

I said, "No, I think I'll stay here for a while."

My partner, Latif, said, "How does it happen you men didn't consult me about reducing the watermelon price?"

I said, "I'm sorry, but we didn't think it was necessary. I'm sure you'll agree with us. We've already spent too much time with the watermelons."

He said, "At least you should have asked me. I'm your partner, aren't I?"

Taib said, "It doesn't really matter. Whatever we do, you're included. You shouldn't take it personally. After all, Larbi was the one who put all the money in. You and I, we didn't put in a franc. We're only in for the profit, not for the loss."

Latif said, "Ouakha, if that's the way you men want it, I'll go along."

I said, "Ouakha, we have to sell all these watermelons in three or four days. I don't think this business is working very well with my other job."

We stayed with the business selling watermelons cheap, today and tomorrow. Four days later, we had sold all the watermelons.

I took back the scale and paid the man who had rented it to us. We counted the money. We had made 30,000 francs profit. We divided it into 10,000 francs apiece.

I said, "Gentlemen, it's been a great pleasure to have you as partners. Thank you very much."

"Allah ihennikoum."

It had taken us five weeks to sell the truckful of watermelons. Each of us went on his way. I decided that was the time to go to the park. On my way to the park, I ran into Lila again.

She said, "Ahilan." I said, "Ahilan."

She said, "I heard you were accusing Fatoma of stealing something from the house."

"Oh, yes, I did. I made a mistake. Everyone makes mistakes. It wasn't my fault."

"How about you and me going to the cinema?"

"No. Thank you. I already told you I don't want to go anywhere with you. I already have enough problems without going out with anybody."

"You don't like me very much, do you?"

"Oh, no, sweetheart, I like you. You're very nice and young and attractive, but I don't want to fool around with anybody. It will bring disgrace to my family. I don't want to have any more problems with my family than I already have."

"I only care for you because Fatoma told me you were a very lonely man."

"I'm not really lonely. I just don't like to go out with people who I don't know."

"Ouakha, I won't ask you again. You're going to be sorry."

"Yes, I've been sorry so many times in my life, it makes

me sick thinking about it."

She said, "Well, I think I'll have to say Allah ihennik, and I don't think I want to bother with you anymore."

She went on her way, and I went on my way to the park. When I got to the park, I found three little girls. They were very young, eleven or twelve. They kept looking at me and smiling. They were talking to each other and giggling a lot. They came to me and said, "We'd like you to buy us some candy."

I said, "No, I don't have any money and I don't want to buy you any candy. Why don't you go away."

I knew that was trouble, buying candy for little girls. People might think I was having something to do with them.

I said, "Go away! Go away! Don't you ever ask grown men to buy you candy!"

I walked away from them, and they kept following me. I decided to go back to town, so people wouldn't think something suspicious was going on. On my way back, in the center of town, I saw Lalla Ann and Haskell coming toward me.

I said, "Good afternoon. Buenas tardes."

They said, "Buenas tardes."

I asked them where they were going. Lalla Ann said she was going back to Tangier. I asked her when she was coming back. She said she didn't know. We stayed there talking, all three of us, until the bus came. We put Lalla Ann on the bus and it took off for Tangier.

7 / Going Back to Tangier

I walked through the Medina and I was thinking. I said to myself, Now the summer is nearly over. I'd better start thinking of what I'm going to do after I go back to Tangier. I should have asked Lalla Ann before she left if she knew anyone who needed help. She knows a lot of people.

I began to think about the two men who had taken my jewelry to Spain to sell. I said to myself, It's been two months. I haven't heard from those men. I don't think I'm ever going to hear from them. I finally realized why Mr. Miles hadn't let those two men sleep in the house.

We stayed in Arcila, today and tomorrow, until the summer ended. One afternoon at the beginning of September Mr. Miles told me we would be going back to Tangier next week. I told him that was fine. The following week we packed all our things and I went downtown and got a taxi. I brought the taxi to the house and we loaded our things and took off for the bus downtown. We took a bus and went back to Tangier. Mr. Miles and I hardly spoke to one another. He was talking to different people and I was talking to different people. When the bus arrived in Tangier, we took a taxi from the Plaza de España to Mr. Miles's apartment. I helped him carry all the things upstairs, and he paid me for that week. I said: "Allah ihennik." I went home. When I arrived home, my wife wasn't there. I wondered where she had gone.

I went to her mother's. Her mother wasn't home. I kept saying to myself, I wonder where she's gone. I'll see her later. Two days later my wife came. I told her, "We are invited to a concert."

A week later I told my wife, "I hope you haven't forgotten that we are going to the concert tonight with Mr. Miles and Lalla Ann."

She said, "No, I haven't forgotten."

"Ouakha, I'm going out for a while. I'll be back by eight o'clock and you should be ready."

I went out for a while and came back home later. My wife was ready. I said, "Let's go to Lalla Ann's apartment, and then all four of us will walk to Brooks Park."

We left the house and walked through the forest until we reached the Spanish Consulate. We walked for a while until we got to where Lalla Ann lived. We took the elevator upstairs. I rang the bell. Habiba opened the door.

She said, "Good evening, Larbi. Are you waiting for Miles and Ann?"

I said, "Yes, they're expecting me."

We waited in the living room a few minutes. Mr. Miles and Lalla Ann came out. They asked, "Are you ready?" I said yes.

We walked to Brooks Park, which wasn't too far from where Mr. Miles and Lalla Ann lived.

We went in and Mr. Miles gave the tickets to a man at the door. There I saw the young man named Paul Manheim. I looked at him and remembered that hot day when he had picked me up. I told my wife and Lalla Ann and Mr. Miles that I knew that man.

"I have to go over and thank him again for that ride on the bad day when I was going to the moussem."

I went to Paul, said, "Good evening," and shook his hand. I asked if he was the one who sponsored this concert.

He said, "Yes, it's me."

I asked him why he was interested in Moroccan music.

He said, "It's very fine music and I've heard it for a long time. I'm trying to take these musicians to America. If the government allows me, I will do it."

I asked him how he got the musicians all the way from the village of Jejouka.

He said, "I rented a truck, drove it there and picked them up."

"Didn't you need a license for the concert?"

He said, "Yes, I made my own ID's and gave the musicians one each. Mysterious things happened when we came into Tangier. A Highway Patrolman followed us. Then a huge tornado came between us and we never saw that policeman again. That was the will of God! If the policeman had caught us, he probably would have given us a huge ticket, confiscated all the instruments and probably the truck, too."

He said, "I have to get the musicians ready." I thanked him again and walked away. I went back to where my wife and Mr. Miles and Lalla Ann were sitting.

Mr. Miles asked my wife if she wanted something to drink. She said no. He asked me and I said I didn't want anything either. Mr. Miles didn't drink. Lalla Ann didn't drink, so none of us had anything to drink.

We sat there. About ten or fifteen minutes later, the music began. The music was very, very loud. People were talking. They couldn't hear one another. Of course I never liked loud music. It did crazy things to my head. We stayed there for a while. My head started shaking with the loud music.

I told my wife, "Get ready, we have to leave. I don't feel comfortable with this loud music."

She said, "No, I'm not going to leave yet. I like this loud music, and I want to stay here a little longer."

"If you stay here, I'm not coming back to pick you up."

"It's all right. I'll stay here and get back by myself."

I said, "Ouakha."

I went back to Paul and thanked him and told him it was very nice music, but loud music didn't agree with me. Lalla Ann said she was tired, too, and wanted to go home. I said, "Ouakha, I'll walk with you."

I said goodnight to Mr. Miles. Lalla Ann and I walked to her apartment. I pushed the button and the elevator came. I put Lalla Ann in the elevator, said goodnight and left.

The farther I went away from the park, the better the music sounded. I went to the other side of the hill, to the large eucalyptus forest. I sat there, lit a cigarette, and enjoyed the music. The wind brought it right to me, the way I like it, nice and soft. I sat there thinking about what I was going to say to my mother-in-law about my wife.

I stayed there for about 30 minutes, all alone in the middle of the forest.

I walked home. I opened the door, and my mother-in-law was still up. She said, "Where is your wife?"

"My wife is still at the concert. She liked the music and decided to stay a little longer."

She said, "What kind of man are you to leave her at a concert with a stranger and come home without her?"

I told her, "I'm sorry, I didn't want to fight with my wife in front of everybody. I told my wife she was fully responsible for herself."

She said, "You are the strangest son-in-law I've ever known. I have three other sons-in-law and they always take care of their wives. I don't know what to say to you."

I said, "You shouldn't say anything to me. Talk to your daughter. You know we've been fighting all the time. I just couldn't stand any more fighting."

I told my mother-in-law, "I'm tired, I'm going to sleep."

She said, "What about my daughter, how could you leave her all alone with strangers?"

"Talk to her when she comes. Ask her if I left her, or if she wanted to stay."

I went to the other room to sleep. It was very late. In the morning, about four or five, I heard a car stop by our house. My wife was talking and laughing. I knew she had had a good time. I got up early in the morning and left the house. I didn't see my wife or my mother-in-law. I went straight to the port.

I stood in line with a lot of other men, waiting for work. We stayed there until about seven o'clock. They called the men they were supposed to call. The rest of us didn't get a job that day. I decided that if I wasn't going to work that day, I should leave. I left the port. I went straight home.

8 / The Maid of Cynthia Bascom

My wife was gone. She went to the market to buy food. Two weeks later, I went to see Mr. Miles.

I went upstairs, rang the bell and a maid opened the door. I asked if Mr. Miles was home. She said he wasn't. He'd gone to the post office. I decided to come back another time to see him. I said Allah ihennik to the maid and took the elevator downstairs. I stepped outside and started walking up the street. I saw Mr. Miles coming from the post office.

I said, "Good afternoon, Mr. Miles."

He said, "Good afternoon."

He said, "Speak of the devil and he will appear."

I said, "Why?"

"Two girls are here and they want us to take them to town. They read one of your stories and are interested in meeting you."

"Sure. Ouakha."

"Why don't you come to my apartment the day after tomorrow. Come about eight o'clock. Then we'll pick them up at their hotel and take them to town."

Two days later I came back to Mr. Miles's apartment about eight o'clock. I went upstairs and rang the bell. The maid opened the door. I asked her to please tell Mr. Miles I was here. She said to sit down and wait.

Lalla Ann came out and asked what I was doing here. I said, "I'm waiting for Mr. Miles. We're taking two girls out."

She said, "Oh, tonight you men are going to be big shots."

"Yes, I think so."

She asked if I wanted anything to eat or drink.

I said, "No, thank you. I just had my dinner."

Mr. Miles came and asked if I was ready. I said yes. We went downstairs. We walked to the taxi stand, in front of the Spanish Consulate, not far away. We took a taxi straight down to the Hotel Minzah. We went inside the hotel. Mr. Miles went to the phone and called the girls. We waited a few minutes. I saw a black girl coming down the stairs. I didn't think she was one of our girls. She came straight to Mr. Miles and said, "Good evening," and he said, "Good evening." He told me this was the girl we were taking out.

I said, "I thought there were two girls."

"Yes, but the other one isn't feeling well, so she can't go out."

"Ouakha."

He introduced me to the black girl, but I forgot her name. I asked them where they'd like to go. Mr. Miles said he knew a cafe where we should go.

We walked down until we got to the U.S. Library, on

the way to the Zoco. We walked through the Zoco all the way down to the Zoco Chico. We kept walking until we got to the Spanish cinema. Behind it there was a huge cafe. We walked in. That cafe was full of men. I never saw so many men in one cafe. Every chair and table looked occupied. There was only one table by the door that wasn't occupied. We took that table, all three of us.

I asked Mr. Miles, "What's so important about this cafe?" He told me to wait and see. The black girl was very excited. She laughed all the time. We ordered three glasses of tea. I saw a stand, like a music stand, on the other side of the hall. Then out came four musicians—two drummers and two pipers. Two boys were dressed in women's clothes. All six of them went to the stand. They began to play music, and the two boys began to dance. Then I knew why the cafe was crowded. The boys shook their bottoms, and every one of us cheered with joy. Almost everyone in the cafe was smoking kif. The more the boys danced, the more excited the men became. I looked around the cafe. It was all smoky. There were waves of smoke near the ceiling. Everybody was cheerful and happy. I looked at everybody, including myself. I knew we were all going to Hell. I knew we were all devils.

We stayed there for a while. The music stopped. All the men began to look at the black lady who was with us. They were winking their eyes at her. She looked like the Queen of Ethiopia to them. As soon as the music started again, they turned their eyes away and looked at the boys dancing. My eyes began to hurt with smoke. The music was making loud echoes. I told Mr. Miles and the black lady, "I can't take this anymore, I have to leave." They decided to leave too. They'd had enough. We left.

We took a taxi, took the black lady back to the Hotel

Minzah. Mr. Miles and I decided to walk home.

I asked, "What does the black lady do?"

"She's a maid. She works for a woman named Cynthia Bascom."

"My God, what a job! Does she take her maid everywhere she goes?"

"Yes, Cynthia Bascom's a very nice lady. She takes her maid everywhere she goes."

"I wish I could get a job like that, so I could travel around the world free."

"Oh, yes, there are lots of people like that in America. They take their maids with them wherever they go. Someday, if you ever go to America maybe you'll find someone like Cynthia Bascom, who'll take you everywhere in the world with her."

We kept walking and talking, until we got to his apartment. I said goodnight and I left.

I went back home. Everybody was asleep. I went straight to bed. Two weeks later I went to see Mr. Miles. I went upstairs and rang the bell. The maid, Meriam, opened the door.

I said, "Good afternoon, Meriam." She said, "Good afternoon."

I asked her if Mr. Miles was home. She said, "No, Mr. Miles went to the post office."

Then I heard the other maid, Habiba, arguing with Lalla Ann. I heard Habiba saying she wouldn't go to the store to buy meat for Lalla Ann's cat, Mimi. They kept arguing and then Lalla Ann came out of the room.

I said, "Good afternoon, Lalla Ann. How are you?" She looked very upset. I asked her, "What were you arguing about?"

She said, "This crazy maid doesn't want to listen to me."

Then Habiba came out screaming: "No, no! I'm not going to the store to buy meat for the cat. She's your cat, not mine."

Lalla Ann said, "Well, you work for me. You're supposed to do what I tell you."

I said to myself, I should go and buy Lalla Ann the meat for the cat and stop all this argument.

I said, "Lalla Ann, I'd like to go to the store and buy the meat for the cat."

"Will you do it?"

"Oh, yes. I'd be very pleased if you'd let me do it."

She gave me the money and I left the apartment. I went downstairs and I started walking down to the boulevard. I walked and walked until I got to the store. I told the man I had come to buy the meat for Lalla Ann's cat.

He said, "Oh, yes, I was waiting for the maid to come and pick up the meat."

He gave me the meat and I paid him. When I was walking back, I started talking to myself. I said, What kind of maid is this girl, that she won't buy the meat for Lalla Ann? If she worked for somebody else, she'd probably be fired on the spot. But Lalla Ann is a very nice lady, she has a soft heart. That's why the maid is giving her a hard time. Then I knew that Habiba had power over Lalla Ann. She wouldn't go to the store to buy meat for the cat.

I walked and I walked until I arrived at Lalla Ann's apartment. I rang the bell and Meriam opened the door.

Meriam said, "Oh, Larbi, that was very fast."

I said, "It doesn't take very long. It just takes a little patience."

Meriam hollered, "Annie! Annie! Larbi's back with the meat."

Lalla Ann came out and thanked me. She was very happy I'd done that little thing for her.

9 / The Library of Congress

I said Allah ihennikoum and walked downstairs. I walked toward the Spanish Consulate and I saw Mr. Miles.

I said, "Good afternoon, Mr. Miles," and he said, "Good afternoon."

I asked him if he had any news about the book.

"Oh, yes. I have a letter here from the Library of Congress." He opened the letter and looked at it. Then he turned around and looked at me.

He said, "Look at this man!" And he looked me straight in the face.

I said, "What's wrong with this man?"

"The Library of Congress wants to have your name, and they want you to send them the tapes of your book."

The more he read the letter, the more upset he looked. I didn't know anything about the Library of Congress—what it is and what it meant.

I said, "Ouakha. Send them the tapes, and you know my name."

Then he walked away from me really fast. He took three steps in front of me and he turned around and said, "Give me your name."

"You know my name. Why are you asking my name—you know it."

I said to myself, I think Mr. Miles wants me to change my name. I better do what Mr. Miles wants.

I said, "Driss Ben Hamed Charhadi."

And that's how the name of Driss Ben Hamed Charhadi came to exist. That was the last thing we said about my name. I didn't take it seriously, that he really wanted me to change my name.

I asked him again if that was all the news he'd heard about the book.

He said, "That's all I know."

I said, "Good afternoon," and I walked away from him. He went home, and I went on my way.

10 / The Port of Tangier

When I got home, my wife wasn't there. I thought that my wife had gone to her mother's. I decided to go to Mustafa's cafe. I walked in. A man asked me if I wanted to play for a glass of tea. I said no.

"What's the matter, are you afraid of losing? It's just for a glass of tea. Can't you afford it?"

I said, "No, I don't want to play for tea. If you want a glass of tea, I'll buy it for you. I don't want to play any cards for tea."

I'd seen men play before for glasses of tea, and when they lost, they just wanted to keep playing. Sometimes they started fighting. I didn't want to play. I stayed there for a little while.

Then Mustafa came. He said, "Ahilan, how are you, Larbi?"

I said, "I'm fine."

He asked me how my job in Arcila was. I told him I didn't work in Arcila anymore.

I said, "I have to start looking for a job tomorrow. Do you know of anyone who needs help?"

"No, I don't. You should go see my brother, Abdeslam. He works down at the port."

"Ouakha, I might just do that."

"Sure. If he has any jobs, you'd be the first one to work."

I decided I was going to leave. He said, "Wait a minute. I'm going home. I'll give you a ride to where I live. That will take you halfway home."

I waited for him while he took care of his business with the man who worked for him. We went to his car and we drove off. I got out at his house and I walked across the field to my house. When I got home, I opened the door and I went in. My wife was still not there. I decided to go to bed. When I woke in the morning, my wife was still gone.

I went down to the port to see if I could find Mustafa's brother and talk to him about a job. I arrived at the port and I began to ask people where Abdeslam worked. A man said, "Abdeslam, he's over there in that big ship. He's trying to sign up a crew."

"How can I get there?"

"You have to go with the workers when the barge comes."

"Where is the barge going to pick up the workers?"

"Right over there in front of the warehouse."

I went there and I waited until the barge came. The man on the barge began to call the names of the men who would work that day. He called and called. I wasn't on the list.

The man looked at me and said, "Where are you going?"

"I'm going to go see Abdeslam."

"Are you a friend of Abdeslam?"

"Yes."

"Ouakha. Get in."

I got on the barge and they hooked the barge to a tugboat and it pulled the barge all the way to the big ship. They hooked up the barge and the men began to climb the stairs, one by one.

I asked one of the men: "Where is Abdeslam?"

He said, "Abdeslam is in the cabin upstairs."

I went to the cabin and I knocked on the door.

Abdeslam said, "Good morning, Larbi."

"Good morning."

"What happened to you? Last time I saw you, you were working in Arcila."

"Yes, I no longer work in Arcila. My job is finished. That's why I'm here this morning—to ask you if maybe you could use some help."

"I'm sorry. Today I've already made the list of all the men who will work. I'll put your name on the list today, and you come and work tomorrow."

I said, "Ouakha," and he put my name on the list for the following day. I waited until the barge was loaded and I got into the barge and the tugboat pulled us to the warehouse. I climbed out of the barge and I went for a walk along the pier. I walked for a while. I was getting hungry. I had to go home. When I got home, I found my wife there.

I said, "Good morning," and she said, "Good morning."

I asked her where she had been last night. She said, "I went to my mother's."

Then she said: "What are you going to do?"

"I don't know. I know I have a job for tomorrow, working down at the port."

"Do you have any money? I owe some money and I need some more for myself."

I gave her 10,000 francs. She said, "That's not enough. I owe 10,000 francs. This won't leave me any."

I gave her another 10,000 francs and told her to be careful with the money. I didn't know if I would be working.

"Don't worry about it, I'll take good care of it. I'll probably spend it in two days!"

I stayed home all the rest of the afternoon. I went to sleep. The following morning I got up early, ready to go to work. I asked my wife if she would be home today.

"Yes. My mother and my sister are coming to visit me."

"Ouakha. I'm going to work and I'll be back this evening. Be sure to have dinner ready when I get home."

"Don't worry. Dinner will be here."

I left and I closed the door. I walked down to the port and I found a lot of people in line waiting for a job. I stood with the men in line and they began to call names. Each person they called walked right to the barge. Finally they called my name. I went to the barge. There were about sixty-five of us. The boat pulled the barge to the big ship. We climbed the stairs. They divided us into four sections. They told everybody to pick out a partner. I picked the man who was standing right in front of me and we went over to the place where we were to work. Men were unloading boxes of machinery. We worked that way, unloading the boxes, until about eleven o'clock that morning. One man said, "Have you men heard the news?"

I said, "What news?"

"The government is going to stop the ships from coming into Tangier, because the port of Tangier is owned by a French company and the Moroccan government wants to build a new port. That's only an excuse so the government can stop ships from loading here. They can transfer all the business to the port in Casablanca."

"Why are they going to do that? Tangier has a big port and Tangier is close to Europe. Spain is right across the ocean. You can see it from here."

The man said, "Well, I hope this isn't true. If this happens, we're all going to lose our jobs."

We heard the whistle for lunchtime. Abdeslam came out of his cabin and said: "Come over here, Larbi."

I went to him and he asked me, "Did you bring any lunch?"

"No, I didn't."

"Well, you can have lunch with me if you want to. I brought enough."

"Ouakha."

He brought his basket of food. He had one loaf of bread, a pot full of chickpeas and a small dish of fried fish. We washed our hands and started eating our lunch. We finished lunch and he said, "Do you want tea?"

"Where can you get tea here?"

"I know the people in the kitchen. We can have tea if you want some."

"Ouakha."

He went to the kitchen and he stayed there for a while. When he came back, he had a big pot full of tea and two glasses. We drank our tea and stayed there talking for a while until the whistle blew and everyone went back to his job.

I asked the same man, "Remember the news we were talking about, about the port—do you know when this is going to happen?"

"No. I heard some very important people talking about it."

We worked all the afternoon until five o'clock. Then Abdeslam came and told all the workers that if anyone wanted to work overtime, he could. If not, he could leave then. Most of the men didn't want to stay. About ten of us stayed until around nine o'clock. The barge came and picked us up and took us to the warehouse. We went to the office and they paid us. I made 8,000 francs that day which was very good.

I was tired and I went straight home. When I got home, I found my mother-in-law, her daughter and her three children. I asked my wife if she had any dinner.

We sat and had our dinner. I told my wife I was very tired. I was going to the other room to go to sleep. I asked her if she would make me some lunch for tomorrow.

She said, "Ouakha. I'll make you some lunch."

I picked up two blankets and a pillow and I went to the other room. I made my bed and I went to sleep.

The following day I got up early. My wife's family had slept overnight and the children were already up. I washed and I got dressed. I asked my wife, "Where's my lunch?"

"Your lunch is in that basket. You've got a piece of roasted meat."

I picked up the basket and I left. I walked straight to the Medina. I got to the port about six-thirty and there were a lot of people waiting to be called. They began to call the names, the same as always. We got into the barge. The tugboat took us to the ship. We climbed up the stairs and went to the hold of the ship and we started working. I saw the same man I'd talked to the day before.

I asked him, "Is there any more news about the port?"

"Yes. I don't think we're going to see many ships coming to Tangier anymore."

Suddenly someone dropped a box. The box was full

of Swiss watches. I could see men running to the broken box and putting them in their pockets. I stood there watching them and the man in charge came down and yelled, "What's happening?"

One of the men told him: "This box broke. All the watches are falling out."

He said, "Put this box on the crane and send it up."

They sent the box up and the man in charge could see watches were missing. He nailed up the box and put it with the other merchandise.

I worked that day the same as the day before. I stayed there working at the port. Some weeks I worked two or three days. Sometimes I only worked three or four days a month. That wasn't enough work, but that was all we could get in those days. Morocco had just gotten independence about seven or eight years earlier. It was a struggle to see who would be in charge. From time to time I saw new inspectors at the port and new managers. That was what the people of the South were waiting for – to put their hands wherever they could. The people in the North had nothing to say about the laws made in the South. The South kept sending people to govern the North. Morocco was becoming integrated. I liked Tangier the way it was before, when it was under International Law. When Tangier was international, there were days when we could see eight or ten ships out in the bay, waiting to be loaded. After independence, there were fewer and fewer ships coming into Tangier.

One afternoon I thought about Lalla Ann and Mr. Miles. I decided to go and see them. I went to their apartment and rang the bell. The maid, Meriam, opened the door.

I said, "Good afternoon, Meriam. Are Mr. Miles and Lalla Ann in?"

"Come on in. The Señora Miles is not here. She's in the hospital. And Mr. Miles went to town."

"Do you know what's wrong with Lalla Ann?"

"She wasn't feeling well, and they took her to the hospital three days ago."

"Which hospital is she in?"

"She's in the California Clinic."

"Well, that's good. That's not very far from where I live. I'll go see her tomorrow."

I said: "Allah ihennik" to Meriam and I left. I went down to Mustafa's cafe. Mustafa wasn't there but I found his brother Abdeslam there. I sat down with him. I ordered a glass of tea and we talked. I asked him if there would be any more work soon.

"No. Right now I don't see any ships. If anything comes up, I'll let you know."

I finished my tea and I told Abdeslam I was leaving, I was going home.

"Me, too. Let's walk to the Zoco and we'll take a bus from there."

We walked to the Zoco. We waited for the bus until the bus arrived, the bus that went up to the Mountain. We rode all the way to Abdeslam's house. I stayed on the bus until we got to the Merkala. I got off. I walked home. When I got home, my wife wasn't home. Each time I didn't find her home I decided she'd gone to visit her family. That was all right.

I was hungry and I decided to make an omelette of fried potatoes, what the Spanish call a tortilla. I fried the potatoes and drained them. I beat the eggs and put the fried potatoes back in the pan. I poured the eggs over them. I covered them for one or two minutes. I flipped them over and let them cook for a minute or so, and they were done. I made two sandwiches. I had my dinner. Then I went to bed.

The next morning I got up early. I made some coffee. I had a piece of toast. I stayed home that day to work in the garden. When I finished my gardening, I picked up a bunch of roses and I went to see Lalla Ann. I went to the clinic and I asked the nurses for Ann Weston. Then I saw Lalla Ann in the corner room, in bed. I walked straight to her and I shook her hand and asked her how she was feeling.

"I feel better today than when I was brought here."

She said, "Are those roses for me?"

"Yes. They couldn't be for anybody else."

I asked her, "How is Mr. Miles?"

"He is fine. Haven't you seen him?"

"No. I went yesterday to see you both. I didn't find him home. Meriam told me that you were here in the hospital."

"I'll probably go home tomorrow or the day after. What are you doing these days?"

"Not very much. Sometimes I work at the port, and that's all I do."

We stayed talking for a while and then I told her I was going home.

I said, "I hope you'll get well enough so we can go down to Merkala beach and take a walk soon."

"Oh, yes! I feel better already and I'm getting well."

I shook her hand and said "Allah ihennik." I went home. My wife was still not home. I said to myself, Since I'm not doing anything, why shouldn't I go see my mother?

I walked all the way to my mother's house. It was on the other side of the hill, on the way to the airport. I got to my mother's house. I knocked on the door; nobody was home. I decided to go back home. I walked home and I cooked my dinner. I made couscous, and my wife still didn't come home. I stayed up late waiting for my wife and she never came. I decided I wasn't going to go out looking for her.

I was getting madder and madder. I didn't know what to do with her. The more I talked to her, the worse she got.

I got tired, so I spread blankets on the floor and I slept.

Three days later I decided to see if Lalla Ann had come home from the hospital. I went to the apartment and I rang the bell. The maid Habiba opened the door.

I said, "Good afternoon, Habiba." I asked her if Lalla Ann and Mr. Miles were home.

"No. They're not home. Ann came back yesterday from the clinic. I think Miles and Ann are going to Spain for two or three weeks."

"I'm glad she's out of the clinic. When she comes home, please tell her I came by and I'm glad she feels better. I hope they have a good trip to Spain."

I said "Allah ihennik" to Habiba and I left. I went down to the port to see if they would know of any work. I asked one man, "Have you seen Abdeslam?"

"Yes, I saw him this morning at the warehouse. Why don't you go and see."

I walked to the warehouse but Abdeslam wasn't there. I saw one ship out there in the bay and I thought: With so many people waiting for jobs, in one day they'll be able to load that whole ship.

11 / I Become a Qahouaji

I decided to go to Mustafa's cafe to see if Abdeslam was there. I walked through the Medina until I got to Mustafa's cafe. I didn't find Abdeslam there, but I found Mustafa.

Mustafa asked me if I was working, and I said, "No, I haven't worked for at least seven weeks."

Then he asked if I wanted to work for him two days a week.

"Ouakha. What am I going to be doing?"

"You'll take the place of the qahouaji who works in the cafe. He usually likes to have one or two days off a week."

"Ouakha."

"I'll pay you 2,000 francs a day, and you have to ask Abdallah which days he's going to be off so you'll know when to work."

"Ouakha." I was glad I had that one or two days a week of work. I walked to the counter. I told Abdallah I would be working for him on his days off.

He said, "I like to have Fridays off and sometimes Sundays. Some weeks I only like to have one day off."

"Ouakha. I'll come on Saturday night and ask you if you want to be off on Sunday. Then we'll go from there."

"Ouakha."

I went back to Mustafa's table and I sat with him. There were a lot of people watching television. Someone was giving a speech. He said that King Hassan was coming to Tangier in the summer.

I said to myself, That's good news. This is the first time the people of Tangier will see the king since Morocco got independence. I hope some good will come out of a visit from the king.

People were very excited about the king coming to Tangier. I left the cafe.

The following Saturday I came to see Abdallah. He said he would be off tomorrow.

"Come at six o'clock and I'll open the cafe for you."

The next day I got to the cafe at 5:30. I waited for Abdallah and he arrived. He opened the door and showed me where everything was. There wasn't much to know. The cafe only served coffee, tea and *café au lait*, only three things. Abdallah told me that if I needed coffee or tea or sugar, I should go to the Soussi on the corner, and tell him to put it on Mustafa's bill.

Abdallah left and I started the fire. A few minutes later, three men came and they wanted tea. I made three glasses of tea and I asked the camarero to give me three chits. He gave them to me. The day was growing and there were more people coming to the cafe. About three o'clock that afternoon, Mustafa came and asked me how I liked my job.

"It's not bad."

He asked me if Abdallah and I had agreed on his days

off. I told him no, we hadn't agreed because Abdallah didn't know for sure which days he wanted off.

He said, "Let me talk to him and see. We'll come to some kind of agreement so you don't have to come every other day to ask him which days he wants off."

Then Mustafa said, "Well, since you know how to do everything and you don't need anything, I'm going to the Zoco Chico to see some people, and I'll see you later."

"What time do you close?"

"We close at ten o'clock every evening, but Abdallah has the key so he'll probably be back later to close up."

Mustafa went on his way and I stayed the rest of the evening. About nine-thirty Abdallah came and asked me how I was doing. I told him I was doing fine. He asked me if I had any problems. I said no, I didn't.

I asked him, "What do you want me to do with the chits?"

"Count the chits and put them in a bag. Put the amount on a piece of paper and put that in the bag, too."

I did what he wanted me to do and I put the bag in a cabinet. He said, "Ouakha. Now we're going to close up."

There were two men there and Abdallah told them: "Gentlemen, we're closing up. You'll have to leave."

The two men left and Abdallah and I closed up and we left. I went on my way, and he went on his way. Four days later, I came back to ask Abdallah about his day off.

He said, "I talked to Mustafa yesterday, and we agreed I would work five days and you would work two. I'm going to be off Friday and Saturday."

"Ouakha. I'll see you tomorrow. Did Mustafa leave any money for me?"

"Yes, he left you 2,000 francs. Here." And I left.

The following day I got up early and I went to work.

I stayed working for Mustafa two days a week — today and tomorrow.

June of 1964 arrived. One afternoon I decided to go see Mr. Miles and Lalla Ann.

I went to Mr. Miles's apartment. I rang the bell. The maid Habiba opened the door.

I said, "Good afternoon, Habiba. I came to see Mr. Miles and Lalla Ann. Are they home?"

I heard Lalla Ann's voice asking, "Who is it?"

Habiba said, "It's Larbi."

Lalla Ann said, "Let him in." Habiba let me in.

I went into the living room and I sat down. A few minutes later Lalla Ann came out. She looked well.

She said, "How have you been? I haven't seen you for a while."

"Fine. I came to see you a while ago, and the maid said you were going to Spain. How was Spain? How was your trip?"

"We had a wonderful time. We went to Barcelona, we went to Madrid, and then we went to Paris for two days. We just came from Paris yesterday."

"I'm glad you had such a good time."

"Did you know Miles had rented a house on the Mountain?"

"How is Mr. Miles?"

"He's fine. He just went out. He'll probably need somebody to work for him."

"Do you know when he's coming back?"

"No. He'll probably get in touch with you."

"That's fine. If I'm not home, he can leave a message with my wife. I'm glad everything is fine. I'm going to leave now. I'm working two days a week in a cafe downtown."

I asked her, "How is Haskell? I haven't seen him since we left Arcila."

"He's fine. He's moving to Tangier next month. He's tired of living in Arcila."

"That's good. Probably Tangier will be better for him than Arcila. I hope to see him soon."

I said: "Allah ihennik." I decided to go see my mother. I hadn't seen her for a while.

I walked to my mother's house. I knocked on the door. I could hear an argument inside. My mother opened the door.

"Ah," she said, "how are you, aoulidi? I haven't seen you for a while."

"I'm fine. How about you?"

"Fine."

I said: "Ahilan" to her husband. I shook his hand. They began to argue. My mother was saying no and my stepfather was saying yes. I didn't understand why they were arguing, saying yes and no, yes and no.

I asked them, "What are you fighting about?"

My mother said, "My husband wants to marry another woman."

"Well, that's not bad. There's nothing wrong with that."

"Oh, yes, there is something wrong with it. He's been my husband all these years, and now he wants to marry another woman. Where is she going to live? We don't have enough money. Why does he need two wives?"

My stepfather said, "You, aoulidi, you like the truth. Why don't you tell your mother to stop fighting with me and let me do what I want."

"Oh, no! Don't mix me up with your problems. You have to leave me out. What do my brother and sister say about this?"

"They haven't said anything. The decision is up to me."

Of course, in Islamic law the man always has the rights. I found it very strange that Islam permits such a thing. My poor mother is the one who has to go through all this. He was a very strange man. He was after this woman. She owned two houses and a big ranch that her husband had left her when he died. My mother's husband was very tall and strong and very handsome. Women went crazy over him. Of course, my mother wanted to keep him to herself.

He said, "I've made up my mind. I'm going to marry her whether you like it or not. There isn't anything you can do about it."

I was getting tired and disgusted with the whole thing. They said, "Oh, no, no. You can't leave. You have to stay for dinner."

I said, "Allah ihennikoum." And I left.

I went back home and I found my wife home.

I said, "Ahilan. How are you? Where have you been?"

"I was at my mother's."

"Why don't you tell me when you're going to your mother's? Who are you married to, me or your mother?"

"What are you trying to do, keep me away from my family?"

"No. I'm not trying to keep you away from your family. Your family is here every single day. A week doesn't go by that there aren't two or three of your family here."

"I can go to see my family any time I want. I don't think you should have any objections to that."

"No. I just want to know where the hell you're going to be, that's all."

She started crying. Every time she did that, she humiliated me. That was the weakest part of me. Every time

I heard a woman cry, I felt sorry. Then I'd always lose the argument.

I went into the other room and I went to sleep. I didn't want to hear anything from her anymore.

12 / A House on the Mountain

I slept until morning. I got up and went to work. I was late. Abdallah was already there and he'd opened up and started the fire.

"What happened to you?"

"I'm sorry, I overslept."

"Now everything is ready for you. We'll see you this evening." And he left.

I stayed that day working. Evening came and Abdallah came back. I counted the chits. Then Abdallah closed and we both left. I went on my way.

Two days later I went to see Mr. Miles. I rang the bell and Meriam opened the door. I shook her hand and asked her how she was doing. I asked her if Mr. Miles was home and she said yes.

"Come on in." I went into the living room and I sat down. In a few minutes Mr. Miles came in.

"Ahilan, Larbi." I said "Ahilan" and shook his hand.

"Do you have any news about the book?"

"Yes. Your book is going to be published the end of the year. You're going to be getting some money very soon. By the way, I've rented a house on the Mountain. How would you like to work for me?"

That was a silly question. He knew I was always looking for work.

"Ouakha. I'll work for you."

"Good."

I asked him how much he would pay me. He said he'd pay me 10,000 francs a week, $20.00.

"When are you going to move up there?"

"I'll be taking some things up next week. By the end of the week I hope to be living up there. You could start working for me next Sunday."

"Ouakha. How can I get there?"

"Next Sunday about four o'clock bring your things here. We'll take a taxi and go up to the house."

"Ouakha. I'll see you next Sunday."

I said to myself: I should go down and see Mustafa and tell him I have a job for the summer.

I left Mr. Miles's apartment and I walked down to the Medina. I went to Mustafa's cafe, but he wasn't there. I asked Abdallah if he had seen Mustafa.

"No, Mustafa should be coming soon. I have to give him all the chits."

I decided to sit and wait for him. I asked Abdallah to make me a glass of tea. I wanted to pay the camarero, but he said no. He said Abdallah wanted me to have the tea for nothing. I said, "Good."

There were four men sitting playing dominoes. I went to their table and watched them playing. The losers were mad and the winners were happy. Nobody likes to lose.

Finally Mustafa came and he said, "Why don't you come over here?" We sat down at a table and I told Mustafa about my new job.

He said, "Ouakha. I'm glad you got yourself a full-time job. Abdallah used to work seven days a week. I guess he won't mind doing that again."

I asked him if he could pay me for the two days he owed me.

He said, "Of course." He gave me 4,000 francs. I said, "Allah ihennik."

I went to the Zoco and I bought some bananas and oranges. I walked to my mother's house. I knocked on the door. My stepfather wasn't home. My mother was alone. I asked her how she was doing. She said she was fine. She said her husband had married that woman yesterday.

I asked her, "Where does she live?"

She said, "She lives in one of her houses. He goes there two or three nights a week."

I could see that my mother was very unhappy about the whole thing, but there was nothing she could do about it.

I told her, "Just take it easy and do the best you can. Try to hold your marriage together."

I stayed there talking to her for a little while. Her husband came home. I shook his hand and said, "Congratulations."

He said, "You're the only one of my sons who understands." He surely knew that wasn't true. He knew that we had never gotten along.

I said, "I'm going to leave."

He said, "Why don't you stay and have dinner with us?"

I said, "No, my wife is waiting. She has dinner cooked already." I left my mother's and I went straight home.

I found my wife's sister there. I said, "How've you been?

How are your husband and the children?"

She said, "Fine."

I asked my wife if she had any dinner cooked. She said yes. She had cooked some lamb. She dished out the food and we had our dinner.

She said, "My sister is going to spend the night here."

I said, "Ouakha."

The following morning I left the house very early. I got down to Mustafa's cafe and Abdallah was already there.

I said, "Good morning, Abdallah. Did Mustafa tell you about my new job? I'm only going to be working here today and tomorrow."

He said, "Ouakha. You take care of the cafe now. I'm going to leave. I'll see you this evening."

I stayed there working all day long. The evening came and Abdallah came. We closed as usual. Abdallah left and I went home.

When I got home, I found my mother-in-law there. I said, "Good evening to you."

She said, "Ahilan, Larbi. Why don't you ever come and see me?"

I said, "Well, you come here all the time. I see you when you're here."

She said, "I'm going to stay here for two or three days."

I said, "Ouakha."

My wife said, "Well, let's have dinner."

I told my wife I'd already had my dinner down at the cafe. She shouldn't have waited. She knew I always ate out if I was out this late.

Then I heard knocking on the door. I wondered who it could be, coming to see us so late. I went out and I opened the door. It was my mother.

I said, "Good evening, Mother. What's wrong?"

She said, "My husband hasn't come home for the last three days. He came home tonight and he stayed for half an hour. Then he said he was going back to his new wife, and stay there two or three days. I told him if he wasn't going to stay the night, I wasn't going to be there. I picked up my things, and here I am."

I said, "Come on in, Mother."

"Aoulidi," she said, "I'm going to have to stay in your house for a little while."

My mother came in and she saw my mother-in-law and her daughter.

My mother-in-law said, "Oh, yes. This is the lady I like to talk to, the one I get along with so well." She was referring to my mother.

I said, "I'm going to sleep. You ladies can talk all night long if you want to." I left them there, I went to the other room, and I went to sleep.

The following morning when I got up, my mother-in-law and my mother had already made a big breakfast. That was the first time in a long time I'd had breakfast at home. They made pancakes with honey and they were delicious.

I finished my breakfast. I told them I was going to work. Then my wife said, "Just a minute! Aren't you forgetting something?"

She said, "I need some money. Now that we're a big family, I need more money."

I gave her 30,000 francs and she said, "This is not enough."

I said, "It's all I have."

She said, "I'm going to send my mother to the Zoco to buy food."

I said, "Ouakha." Before I left I told them not to wait for me for dinner that night. I went to work.

When I got there, Abdallah wasn't there. Then he arrived and opened the door. He said, "Allah ihennik, I'll see you this evening."

He left and I did my work that day the same as every other day. In the evening Mustafa came. He said, "Larbi, are we going to see you again?"

I said, "Of course. I'll come by and visit from time to time. I might go down to Merkala, to the cafe."

We stayed, Mustafa and I, talking. Abdallah came and he asked me if I was ready to close. There was no one in the cafe except the three of us.

I counted the chits and put them in a bag. I asked Mustafa to pay me for two days of work. He paid me 4,000 francs. Abdallah closed the cafe. Mustafa said he would give me a ride as far as his house.

We drove away. I got out at his house. I walked to my house. When I got home, I found my stepfather there, asking my mother to come home. My mother was arguing with him. She didn't want to come home unless he got rid of the other wife. He said he didn't want to do that; he'd just got married, how could he get rid of her so soon? They argued back and forth. Finally my mother decided to go back home.

They left. I told my wife I had a new job. "I'm going to be working on the Mountain this coming Sunday. I'll be coming home two days a week."

She said, "What about me? What am I going to do?"

I said, "I don't know. Do whatever you want. You're hardly home anyway."

Three days later Sunday came. I picked up some clothes and I told my wife, "Allah ihennik. I'm leaving. I'll see you next week."

I went to Mr. Miles's apartment. I rang the bell and

Habiba opened the door. She said, "Larbi, what do you have in there?"

I said, "Just some clothes."

She said, "Are you going to be working for Ann and Miles this year?"

I said, "Yes."

She said, "Come on in. Come on in."

Lalla Ann came from the other room. She said, "Are you ready to go to the Mountain?"

I said, "Yes. I'm ready."

She said, "Miles will be here in a minute. Sit down and make yourself at home." She told Meriam to give me something to drink.

Mr. Miles came in a few minutes later. He called a taxi and we loaded the luggage into the elevator and took it downstairs. The taxi came, and we loaded all the luggage into it. We got in and the taxi took off for the mountain. We drove northwest of Tangier up a winding road. The eucalyptus trees smelled nice. There were hardly any cars on the road.

The house was huge. Mr. Miles told the driver that that wasn't the house he'd be living in. The taxi-driver opened a gate and Mr. Miles told him to follow the road to the foot of the hill. A man owned both houses. There was a big garden and the taxi drove through the garden until we reached the house.

We began to carry our things into the house. Mr. Miles paid the driver and told him to close the gate, and to be careful because there was a dog out there. The house was right on top of the cliff. You could stand there and see Spain.

Mr. Miles said, "You take that room by the door and I'll take the one in back. The other two rooms we'll leave for Ann and the maids."

My room had an old bed. The springs were showing. I decided to take the springs out and put the mattress on the floor.

I asked Mr. Miles, "What do you want me to do?"

He said, "You have to watch over the house, and go shopping once or twice a week."

I said, "Ouakha, that's not bad." I asked him, "Am I going to have any days off?"

He said, "Yes, you'll have two days off a week. You have to find somebody to stay here on your two days off."

I said, "Ouakha, I'll find somebody. Next time I go to town I'll look for this man who I think will be willing to work."

Next morning Lalla Ann and her two maids came up. Meriam was supposed to do the house-cleaning, but Habiba didn't do very much. All she did was put her hands in her pockets and walk around.

I said, "Good morning, Lalla Ann. You seem to be here very early."

She said, "Yes. We came to get the house clean. There's a doctor coming from Chicago to see Miles."

I said, "What kind of doctor is he?"

She said, "He's studying all the religions of the world."

I said, "Well, that's good. I'm glad you all came. It gets very lonely here on this mountain." I asked her if she wanted to go on a little walk on the Mountain.

She said, "Of course I'm interested. This afternoon when we finish our work we'll probably go."

I said, "Ouakha. I think I'm going down to the ocean. I'll be back."

13 / The King Is Coming to Tangier

I walked down the cliff and I found some men fishing for lobsters. I stayed there talking to them until about one o'clock. Then I walked up to the house. When I got there, they already had cooked lunch. I went to the kitchen. I took a piece of bread and a couple of strips of liver, and I made a bocadillo. I thanked Meriam and I went out to the garden. I sat and had my lunch. I went back to the house. Lalla Ann asked me:

"Did you know the King is coming in two weeks?"

I said, "So soon?"

She asked me if I was going to see the King. I said I was going down to the city on Friday anyway. I would probably stand around with everybody else and watch the King. I'd never seen the King before.

I said, "Are you ready to go for a walk in the forest?" Lalla Ann said, "Yes. Let's go."

It was silly for me to ask her if she wanted to see the

forest because we were surrounded by forest. Any way you looked there were flowers and eucalyptus and pines, and life was full of green.

We walked through the garden to the fence. I opened the gate and we walked to the right through the forest. We walked for a while. Then we decided to come back home.

She said, "This is beautiful country. I wish we could buy a house up here."

When we got to the house, Lalla Ann said she wanted to take a nap. She would be ready for dinner.

She said, "Are you going to go anywhere this afternoon?"

I said, "No, I'm just going to stay here." There wasn't much for me to do.

I walked through the garden. There were fruit trees there, pears and apples and apricots. My favorite thing was the blackberries. I used to pick them and make jelly with them. They tasted so good. I picked a half-basket, probably a kilo and a half, of blackberries. I brought them home and Lalla Ann was already in the kitchen getting dinner ready.

I said, "Look what I brought for you."

She said, "Where did you get those blackberries?"

I said, "They're all over the garden, everywhere you go. Along the fence you'll find blackberries. I'm going to take these and make some jelly and bring it to the house."

I went to my room and stayed there for a while. Then Meriam came and told me that dinner was ready. All five of us ate at the table and Meriam served the food. She served pinchitos, broiled lamb on skewers. It was delicious. I asked who had made it. Ann said she had.

"How did you make it?"

"I took some olive oil and garlic, a little paprika and white pepper and marinated the meat overnight."

I said, "That's why it tastes so good. You have to show me how to do it."

We had our dinner and then Meriam made tea. Meriam cleaned up and I went back to my room. Lalla Ann and Meriam and Habiba stayed there for three days.

One afternoon in the following week a taxi pulled up to the house. It was the doctor who studied all the religions. That evening we were eating dinner and Mr. Miles didn't offer the doctor anything. I offered him half my dinner. I said to myself, This is a very strange custom. A person comes to the house and he isn't offered any food. We had pinchitos again, that Lalla Ann had sent up with the taxi driver. They were delicious, as always. We finished our dinner and I made tea. Mr. Miles said he didn't want any. I put some mint in the tea and gave the doctor a glass. Mr. Miles and the doctor went to the living room and sat there talking. Two hours later a taxi came and blew its horn. The doctor shook Mr. Miles's hand and shook mine. He got in the taxi and drove away.

The next day was my shopping day. I walked all the way down the hill. I took the bus downtown. I remembered I had to find the man who was going to be working on the weekends. I went straight down to Mustafa's cafe. I found Abdallah there. I asked him if he'd seen Ahmed.

"Which Ahmed are you talking about?"

"The brother-in-law of Mustafa. I have a job that he may be interested in."

We were talking, Abdallah and I, and suddenly Ahmed walked in.

I said, "There he is. Speak about the devil and he will be with you."

I walked to Ahmed and said, "Ahilan. How are you? Are you working?"

He said, "No, I'm not working."

I said, "Would you be interested in working two days a week, up there where I work?"

"What would I do?"

"Not very much. Just watch the house, make sure nothing is stolen."

He said, "Ouakha. I need some money to go to France. I have a job there."

"When are you going to France?"

"In two or three months."

"How did you get a job in France?"

"The French government has a contract with the Moroccan government. Whenever they need people to work in France, they ask the Moroccan government."

"How did *you* get a job?"

"I knew someone in the unemployment office. They select people to go to France."

I thought: The people who go to France are the lucky ones in Tangier because they've been selected for a job.

He asked me, "Where is the house where I'll be working?"

I said, "It's up on the Mountain. The only way you can get there is by walking. You could take a taxi, but a taxi would take all your wages away."

"Where can I meet you?"

"Tomorrow morning at eight o'clock come to Merkala. I'll meet you at the Soussi's, and we'll walk up from there."

He said, "Ouakha. This is great. I'll see you tomorrow."

I went to the market and bought what we needed. I took the bus to Merkala and from there I walked uphill. That was the hardest part of my job, to walk the two miles uphill. I walked and I walked on the winding road. When I got home, Mr. Miles said, "Why did it take you so long?"

I said, "Why don't you try walking uphill—then you'll see what it's like."

He said, "Oh, yes, I know what it's like. We used to live on top of a hill when we first came to Tangier."

I told him, "I found the man I was telling you about. He wants to work here."

"Do you know him? Do you trust him?"

"I know him. I don't know about trust. You never know what people are going to do until they do it."

"When is he coming?"

"He's coming tomorrow morning. I'm meeting him at the foot of the hill."

"Do you know where he lives?"

"He lives down in Dradeb. That's not very far from here. It will be easy for him to walk to work."

The next morning I got up early. I walked down to the Soussi's. Ahmed was already there. He saw me and I waved to him. We walked and walked to the house.

He said, "This is a very long way to walk."

"You only come on Saturday morning. You'll only come uphill once a week."

Ahmed and I walked. We got to the gate and we walked through the garden.

Ahmed said, "What a big garden this is!"

"Yes, it's nice. Up here you could get lost."

"Now I know what you mean. He needs a guard up here."

I opened the door and asked him to come in. Mr. Miles was sitting on the terrace. We walked through the house to the terrace. I introduced Ahmed to Mr. Miles and I told both of them that I was going out for a while. I left them both sitting on the terrace.

A little bit later Ahmed started calling to me. He said,

"We reached an agreement. I'm going to work here two days a week. You can go home and come back Monday morning."

Ahmed wanted to go back home and get some things. We walked back down the hill. I went on my way and he went on his way. When I got home, I found my wife's family there. There were two of her sisters and four children.

I said, "Good morning to you all. How are you all doing?"

My wife said, "I need some money."

"Ouakha." I gave her 18,000 francs. "The money is for one week."

"What am I going to do for one week? I need more money now that the family is here."

"Ouakha. I'll give you some more money next week when I get paid."

I spent two days at home. I went up to the Mountain. When I got there, Ahmed was ready to leave.

I said, "How is everything?"

He said, "Fine."

Mr. Miles paid Ahmed and he left. I stayed there, today and tomorrow. Friday was the day for me to go shopping. I picked up the basket and told Mr. Miles I was going shopping.

He said, "Buy what you need for the food. I need some cigarettes, English cigarettes."

I walked downhill and waited for the bus. The bus was loaded with people who were coming to see the King. People were jammed like sardines. I knew I couldn't get into the bus. I decided to walk, and I walked toward the city. There were hundreds of people walking toward the city. I didn't feel bad because there were so many people walking.

I walked until I got to the top of the Boulevard Pasteur.

I saw the street was full of sand. I asked a man, "Why does the street have sand on it?"

"It's for the King's horses. They won't slip and fall."

I walked all the way down the boulevard to the Zoco. Both sides of the street were full of people. Thousands and thousands of people were waiting for the King to go down to the Grand Mosque. About twelve-thirty the King drove in his limousine to the top of the boulevard. Then he got out and mounted his horse. He rode through the streets where the people were waiting. He waved with his hand and people waved back at him. The people looked cheerful. I wanted to follow the King down to the Grand Mosque, through the Medina down to the Zoco Chico.

I walked through the Zoco Chico and there was one policeman every ten yards. Nobody could cross the street. You could only walk on one side of the street. I kept walking until I got very close to the Grand Mosque. I went up to the Spanish Terrace and I saw that the roof of the Grand Mosque was full of Secret Police. There were police on both sides of the street. There was one thing missing that Friday. There were no beggars in the street for the King's visit. That's why they chased the beggars away. On Friday Moslems give money away to the beggars in Tangier. This way the King would think, there are no beggars in Tangier, no poor people.

I walked to the Mosque; I wanted to get in. The police said, "Do you have permission?"

I said, "No, I don't have permission. I always come here on Friday."

"You do, but not today. Only special people who have permission get in today."

I decided to go back to the terrace and watch all the people waiting for the King. About forty minutes later, the people began to leave the Mosque. The King stepped out of the Mosque, and his horse was waiting for him. He mounted the horse and they started up through the Zoco Chico toward the Zoco de Fuera. I saw hundreds and hundreds of people handing letters to the King. The police tried to push people back, to keep the people from giving the King letters. The people kept giving letters to the King, and he handed them back to his escorts. I kept following them all the way until they reached the boulevard. The King got off his horse and got into his limousine. People kept running to him and giving him letters. The police tried to keep the people away from the King.

The King drove to the top of the boulevard. I ran faster and faster, five or six blocks ahead of the King. When I got there, I saw the meanest policeman in Tangier. He was hitting men over the head with his club, trying to show the girls what a big man he was.

I said to myself, I wish the King could see this. People came from a long way to see the King, and here's a policeman oppressing people.

I stood there watching the policeman beating the men. The King was getting closer. The policeman stopped. He stood on the sidewalk as the King was coming toward him. There were more people giving letters to the King. They were all crying for justice.

I went farther up the street and there were no police. There were soldiers with machine guns. Every ten yards there was a soldier. It reminded me of the days of the revolution. There were thousands and thousands of soldiers. They stood in a line all the way from the boulevard to the Mountain where the King's palace was.

I said to myself, Well, now I've seen the King. I think I'll go back down to the Zoco and do my shopping. Then

I'll go back to the Mountain.

I tried to cross the street, and a policeman from the Rif wouldn't let me go. I told him I had to go down to the Zoco to shop for my boss.

He said, "I don't care about where you work or who you work for. No one is allowed to cross the street until the King leaves."

I said, "Look, my good man, if I don't go shopping and return to where I work, my boss is not going to like it."

"Look here, I don't care who you work for. The rules are the rules for everyone."

I stood there waiting for the King to leave. Finally he left, and people began to leave. I left with them. I walked down to the Zoco and I did the shopping. I went to the bus stop and waited for the bus. It never came.

I asked the dispatcher if there would be any buses today. He said no, there wouldn't be any buses until tomorrow.

I decided to walk home. There were hundreds of people walking home. When I got to the foot of the Mountain, I rested for a while. I started walking. When I got home, I told Mr. Miles what had happened.

He said, "Oh, yes, I see. Now I know why you're late."

I saw a man sitting with Mr. Miles. I said good afternoon and he said good afternoon.

Mr. Miles said, "This is a friend of mine. His name is Abdallah. He came to visit me from Marrakesh."

I shook the man's hand. Then he said, "What do you do here?"

I said, "I work here. I'm the houseboy."

"Aren't you ashamed of yourself? Only women do that kind of work."

He made me really mad. I asked him what kind of work

he did.

"Me? I don't do any work. All I do is visit friends. I never met a man like you who does women's work."

I told him to behave himself. I'd had a bad day. Did he come all the way from Marrakesh to criticize me?

I asked him, "What do you think I should do for a living?"

"I don't know. You should get a job like other men."

I said, "Why don't you mind your own business and let me do mine?"

I took the food to the kitchen and put everything where it's supposed to be. I told Mr. Miles I was going to walk down to the sea. I stayed there for a while, and then I came back home. I prepared dinner for all three of us. We had our dinner, and I made tea. I didn't talk to the man all through dinner.

He stayed with us three days. The third day Mr. Miles said: "You have to take him down to the train station."

I said, "No, I'm not going to take him to the station. He's your friend, he's not my friend. He came on his own, why can't he leave on his own?"

"I want you to take him down to the train station."

We kept arguing back and forth. I finally decided I would take him to the train.

I told the man: "Come on, let's go." We walked and walked until we got to the foot of the Mountain. Then we took the bus to the Zoco. We got off and started walking down to the station. It was on the east side of the city. I didn't say a thing to the man, all the way to the station. When we got there, I told him to buy his ticket and wait for the train.

I said, "Allah ihennik. Good luck to you."

That was the first and the last time I ever saw him.

I walked through the Medina to the Zoco. Then I caught a bus going to the Mountain. When we got there, I got off the bus and started walking uphill. I walked until I got home. I told Mr. Miles I'd taken the man to the station.

Three days later Friday came. I told Mr. Miles I was going to do the shopping. I walked down to the foot of the hill. That Friday there were plenty of buses. I took a bus to the city. I walked through the Medina all the way to the Grand Mosque. On both sides of the street there were beggars sitting, waiting for people to leave the Mosque. That was the way it usually was on Fridays.

14 / Crying for Justice

I went inside the Mosque and sat. The speaker stood up and began to speak about justice and Islam. We began to say the prayer. When we finished the prayer, one man stood up in the middle of the Mosque crying, "Allah, give me justice!"

Everyone turned around and looked at him, and asked him what was wrong. He just said, "Allah!" He didn't say anything else. I tried to go to him and ask him why he was crying for justice. By the time I got there, he was gone. When people stand up in the middle of the Mosque and cry out for justice, there's hardly any justice given to them. I knew that man was very hurt. That's why he was crying for justice.

I left the Mosque with everybody else. On my way out, I heard people speaking about justice. They were saying that when the French and Spanish were ruling Morocco, there was more justice than we have now. At least the French treated everyone equally under the law. Now we have our own government and one can hardly speak the truth. New laws have been made that people can't understand.

I walked away from the Mosque, through the Zoco Chico up to the Zoco de Fuera. I went to the market and bought all the food we needed. I went to the bus stop and waited for the bus. I rode up to the foot of the Mountain. I started walking from there.

When I got to the house, Mr. Miles asked me if I had gotten everything.

I said yes. He said, "Don't forget Ann and Habiba are coming this evening. They're bringing dinner."

I said, "I didn't forget. What time are they coming?"

"Between six-thirty and seven o'clock."

I took the food to the kitchen. I decided to go down to the sea for a while. I walked down the cliff and I stayed by the shore. When I came up, there were five people in the house talking to Mr. Miles.

I said good evening and they said good evening. I went to the kitchen and made tea. I asked them if they wanted some tea. They said no, they were drinking.

I took my tea to the terrace and I stood watching the sea and ships going toward Gibraltar. It began to get dark. The people told Mr. Miles they were going to leave. It was between seven and eight, and we waited for Lalla Ann and Habiba. They didn't come.

I began to worry about why they were so late. I decided to walk to the foot of the hill to see what was happening. I walked down the hill. It was dark — you couldn't see your fingers in front of you if you put them straight out. I walked until I was almost halfway down the Mountain. I heard people talking. The closer I got, the clearer the voices became. It was Lalla Ann and Habiba, walking up the hill with two baskets full of food. They were talking — they were really mad.

I said, "Ann! Habiba!"

They said, "Who's that?"

I said, "Larbi."

Lalla Ann said, "Oh, thank God you came to meet us!"

I took the two baskets and I asked Habiba what happened.

She said, "Do you want me to tell you what happened?"

"Ouakha, what happened?"

"You two grown men sitting in the house and we two women bringing you food and you don't even care what happens to us! Who do you men think you are?"

"I'm sorry, but you still haven't told me what happened."

"We took a taxi from the Spanish Consulate and he took us halfway up the Mountain and he was stuck. He couldn't go any higher. That's what happened."

"Well, I'm sorry. I didn't know what happened. Will you please stop complaining!"

"No!"

Finally Lalla Ann told her: "Shut up! Be quiet! He didn't know this was going to happen. How could he have known? At least he's here."

Habiba kept talking and Lalla Ann kept telling her to be quiet. But Habiba couldn't stand to be quiet. This was her opportunity to tell me anything she wanted.

We walked and walked until we got to the house. When we got there, Mr. Miles asked Ann what happened. She told him about the taxi. Then Habiba jumped again.

"You two men sit there and you don't care what happens to us!"

Mr. Miles said, "Be quiet! I didn't know anything had

happened to you. Be quiet!"

Then I really saw Habiba the way she was. She was a very strange woman. For the first time I saw that Lalla Ann and Mr. Miles were afraid of her.

Then Ann and Habiba went to the kitchen. They warmed up the food and set the table and we ate our dinner. When we finished, I picked up the dishes and went to the kitchen and made tea. We all had our tea. Then I helped Habiba with the dishes.

I went to my room and I began to think about Habiba—the way she treated Lalla Ann and Mr. Miles. I said to myself, Look how some people can be so fortunate. They can say anything to the bosses, and nothing will ever happen to them. If that was me, I'd probably already be kicked out.

Finally, I fell asleep.

The following morning I got up early. I went for a walk in the forest. When I came back, Lalla Ann had already made breakfast. She'd made jam from the blackberries I'd collected for her. There was toast with butter and jam and it was delicious. That jam was delicious. It was the best jam I ever had in my life.

Lalla Ann said, "You men will have enough jam to last you until the end of the summer."

I finished my breakfast and I decided to go down to the sea. I told them I would see them later.

Mr. Miles said, "Ann and I are going for a walk in the forest. When you get back, we probably won't be here."

I said, "That's all right."

I walked down the cliff until I got to the sea. I saw two men fighting for one fishing spot. They were arguing back and forth about which one had the right to the place. When I got to them, I said good morning. They both said good morning at the same time.

I said, "Why are you fighting over this spot? What's so special about this spot?"

One of them said, "This is my spot and I come and fish here every day."

The other one said the same thing.

I knew they were both lying because I had never seen either of them there before.

I said, "You shouldn't fight for this special place. The sea is very big. It all depends on which of you is lucky. That one will get the fish."

They were fighting over that spot because there was a big rock there that you could climb up on and you could fish very comfortably. Finally one of them decided to fish somewhere else. He picked up his bucket and went to the other side of the hill.

I sat there watching them fish without catching anything. I said to myself, There you go. If your day starts with bad luck, nothing goes right.

I walked up the steep hill. When I got to the house, there was only Habiba alone in the house. I said to myself, I think I'm going to find out how much Habiba cares for Lalla Ann.

I asked Habiba to make some tea. I said, "Come out on the terrace. I want to talk to you."

She said, "What do you want to talk about?"

"Bring the tea and come to the terrace and we'll talk."

"Ouakha."

She went to the kitchen and made tea. She filled two glasses and came out to the terrace and sat down.

I asked her. "Do you love Lalla Ann as much as Lalla Ann loves you?"

She said, "A little bit. I care for Ann. I couldn't say

I love her. I like young girls. I like to sleep with younger girls. Ann is an older woman. Young girls make me feel alive, they give me lots of energy and they always do what I tell them to. I've been working for Ann for a long time. I need to work for Ann so I have enough money to take girls out. They think I'm very rich."

I knew that Lalla Ann wasn't any older than Habiba. I knew that Habiba was abusing Lalla Ann for her own selfish reasons.

I said, "What would happen to you if Lalla Ann fired you?"

"Ann couldn't fire me. I have her where I want her. Anyway, if she fires me, I'll go back to my wheat business. I was doing well before I met Ann."

"You couldn't do that well. Lalla Ann gave you her house. She pays you well. You hardly do any work and you're supposed to be a maid."

"Oh, yes, when I first met Ann I worked as her maid. But not anymore. Now we have the other maid to do all the work in the house. Not me. Me, I've already made my money. All I do is go with Ann. She can't go anywhere without me. She needs my help."

"Why does she need your help?"

"Because Ann is crazy."

"That's not true. There's nothing wrong with Lalla Ann. How could you say she's crazy?"

I knew that wasn't true at all. She was trying to escape from the truth.

I asked her: "Are you going with anyone else right now besides Lalla Ann?"

"Yes. I see a girl from time to time. She's very young and very beautiful."

I told her: "I'd like to meet the girl." I wanted to find

out what was really going on.

She said, "Sure. Come to my sister's house and I'll take you with me and show you the girl."

About eleven o'clock Ahmed came. He called, "Ahilan. Ahilan. Is anyone home?"

I said, "Ahilan, Ahmed. You were late this morning. What happened?"

He said, "I sent down to the Medina to see if my contract had arrived from France."

"Did it?"

"Not yet. There are two hundred of us that are going to Paris. Our contracts haven't arrived yet."

"Are you really going to France?"

"Yes. I've got my passport all ready. All we're waiting for are the contracts."

"Ouakha. You're here now. Take care of things. I'm leaving."

I went to my room and I picked up my things. I said "Allah ihennikoum" to Ahmed and Habiba, and I left. On my way out to the gate, I saw Lalla Ann and Mr. Miles coming back. I told Mr. Miles I was going home for a couple of days. He asked if Ahmed had arrived.

I said, "Yes. He's at home with Habiba."

I thanked Lalla Ann again for that wonderful jam she'd made. I said "Allah ihennikoum." I walked down the hill.

When I got home, I found the house full of people. There were my mother-in-law, her daughters and her grandchildren. I went crazy with all these people in the house. The harder I worked, the less money I had.

I asked my mother: "How are you, how's your husband, how are my brother and my sister?"

She said, "They're all fine."

"How is your husband's new wife doing?"

"Aoulidi. You don't know what happened!"

"No."

"My husband has already divorced that poor lady."

"So soon?"

"Yes. He sold her ranch in the country and one of her houses in the city. He grabbed all her money and divorced her and sent her away."

"How do you feel about it?"

"I feel good. I like to have my husband all to myself. I know that's not possible. The husband is the master. He does whatever he pleases and Islam backs him up."

My mother looked happier. I knew that wasn't going to last for very long. I'd seen him before breaking her heart, and she didn't do anything about it. She was crazy with love with him. When she had him all to herself, it was a blessing.

Two hours later, my mother-in-law's mother came to the house. She was an old lady. She wanted to stay for a few days.

15 / The Holy Man

My mother-in-law began to talk about the King. Her son-in-law, Abdallah, had worked for the King's family for all the time he was in Tangier. Abdallah said the King was the gentlest person he had ever met.

I said, "That's good. I'm glad someone thinks the King is a good man."

I thought: I want to get away from all this noise. I think I'll go down to the Medina and see if I can escape from it.

I told them I was leaving and I didn't know when I was going to be back. I told them please not to wait for me to have dinner.

I left the house and I started walking. I walked all the way to the Spanish Consulate. I waited there for the bus. I took the bus down to the Zoco. When I got there, there was a holy man with a big beard saying: "Ladies and gentlemen – don't drink Coca Cola. Coca Cola is made from pig's blood."

Since Moslems don't eat pork, it was the only way to get them not to drink Coca Cola. It was the holy man's job to announce that Coca Cola wasn't good for Moslems. I thought this was a crazy idea—how could they put pig's blood in Coca Cola?

He kept walking down the street and many children were following him. Even adults stopped to listen. They began to talk to one another. They said, "Yes, yes. It's not clean. It's a sin to drink Coca Cola because it's made with pig's blood."

I walked away from the crowd and began to walk toward Mustafa's cafe. I wanted to find some people to talk to. When I got there, I asked for a glass of tea. There was no one there I knew. Mustafa wasn't there. The camarero brought my tea and I asked him about what the man on the street had said—that Coca Cola was made with pig's blood.

He said, "Yes. That's what we heard. That's why we're not selling any Coca Cola in the cafe."

"Do you personally believe that Coca Cola is made with pig's blood?"

"I don't know. I don't drink it very much anyway. You like Coca Cola sometimes, don't you?"

"Yes, I do."

"You'd better not let anyone catch you drinking it now! If someone sees you drinking Coca Cola, they'll say you're a traitor to Islam."

This was happening right after Independence. Everyone had new ideas about how to get rid of the Coca Cola Company.

I stayed there until I finished my tea and then I left the cafe. I went up through the Zoco de Fuera to the Mendoubia. There were five American girls there. They were tall and slender and they all had blond hair. There was a big box in front of them filled with ice and Coca Cola. They were giving away free bottles of Coca Cola to people. They said: "Here. Taste. Coca Cola doesn't taste like pig's blood, does it?"

Nobody wanted any because the holy man had already spoken against it.

I got closer and closer to them. By the time I got in front of them, those girls looked very attractive. They were smiling at people who were watching them. They kept handing out the Coca Colas but none of the people wanted any. They just stared at the girls. Finally one of the girls handed me a Coca Cola and I took it. Everyone looked at me and said: "Look at him! He's a devil!" I started drinking. They said: "He's drinking pig's blood!" Some of them said: "Stay away from him! Stay away!"

The Coca Cola was very refreshing. I finished it and asked them for another one. I asked them if I could take it without opening it, and they said, "Sure." I walked away.

The following day I came back to the same spot. I saw a few people drinking Coca Cola. The same girls were there giving it away free of charge. I asked them for a Coca Cola. They gave me one to drink, and then they gave me six bottles to take with me. I took the Coca Colas and I went straight home.

When I got home, my grandmother-in-law and my mother had both already left.

I asked my wife: "Do you have my things ready?"

She said, "Yes. Everything is in your bag."

I picked up my bag and I said: "Allah ihennikoum." I left. I decided to go down to the Medina to see Habiba. I walked until I got to the neighborhood where Habiba lived. I knew where she lived because I used to know her nephews.

I went and I knocked on the door. Habiba's sister came out. I said, "Ahilan," and she said, "Ahilan."

She said, "Who are you?"

"I'm Larbi. I work for the lady named Ann, the one your sister works for. Habiba told me to come and see her."

"Habiba's not here. She's at Ann's house if you want to see her."

"Well, it doesn't matter. I'm going up there anyway."

Then this young, very attractive girl came to the door looking for Habiba. I said, "Ahilan," and she said, "Ahilan." I asked her if she was looking for Habiba. She said, "Yes."

I said, "Habiba's not here. I was looking for her myself. What is your name?"

"My name is Saida. What is your name?"

"I'm Larbi."

"Where do you know Habiba from?"

"We work for the same person."

"Oh, yes. You're the watchman at the mountain house."

"That's me. Where do you know Habiba from?"

"I've know Habiba for a long time. We're very close friends."

"How close?"

"We're very close. Habiba helps me a lot. She buys me very expensive gifts."

When she said that, I remembered what Habiba had said about the girl she was going out with. I finally realized that Saida was the girl she was talking about.

I said, "Allah ihennik. If I see Habiba, I'll tell her you're looking for her."

I started walking toward the Mountain. I got home. Habiba and Lalla Ann were still there. They were all sitting and drinking tea. Mr. Miles and Ahmed weren't there.

Lalla Ann asked me: "How was your weekend?"

I said, "It was nice."

She asked me if I wanted any tea and I said, "No, thank you."

I wanted to talk to Habiba alone but I couldn't. I wanted to tell her that I had seen her girlfriend and now I knew what she meant when she said she was a very beautiful girl.

Then Lalla Ann said, "Larbi, did you know Haskell has already moved to Tangier?"

I said, "No."

"Yes. He got an apartment in front of the Spanish Park. It's on the way to your house."

She described the building to me and I knew it.

I said, "Oh, that's good. I might go to see him tomorrow on my way to buy food. I haven't seen Haskell since Arcila."

I told the ladies I was going for a hike. I asked them if they wanted to go. They said they were all too tired. I left.

I went to the forest, and I walked and walked.

When I got back home, they had already cooked dinner. We ate dinner and Habiba made tea. Mr. Miles told me that Ahmed had wanted to talk to me but he had left. I told him that was all right with me.

I went to my room and after a little bit I went to sleep.

The next day I got up early. Lalla Ann was already up. She and Habiba were in the kitchen making breakfast.

Lalla Ann said, "You're up early."

"Not as early as you two."

"You want breakfast?"

They made scrambled eggs and toast with jam. They filled a glass with tea. I went to the terrace and had my breakfast.

Lalla Ann asked me: "What are you going to do today?"

"I'm going shopping and I think I'll go and see Haskell."

"Why don't you wait for us? We're going to get a taxi."

"No, thank you. I like to walk in the morning. I'm going downhill. It's easy."

I went to the kitchen and picked up the basket. I started down the hill until I got to the American Consulate. I walked to the Spanish Park and to the Big Villa where Haskell lived. I rang the manager's bell, and a Spanish woman came out. I told her I was looking for a man named Haskell Josephs.

She said, "Oh, the American."

"Yes."

"He lives upstairs in apartment number 3."

It was a big villa they had developed into apartments. I walked up to number 3 and I rang the bell. I heard dogs barking. I said to myself, This has got to be Haskell's apartment.

A voice said, "Who is there?"

I said, "Larbi. Larbi."

Then Driss opened the door.

Driss said, "Oh, good morning, Larbi."

I said, "Good morning. Is Haskell here?"

Haskell came out. "Oh, good morning, Larbi. How have you been? We haven't seen you for a long time."

I said, "I'm fine. When did you move to this apartment?"

"About two weeks ago."

"How do you like Tangier?"

"I don't know yet. Why don't you sit down and we'll make tea."

I sat down and Driss made tea for all three of us.

Haskell said, "You know what?"

I said, "No. What?"

"I have a check here for you for $100. Ann told me where you lived, and I was going to bring it by, but I haven't had time. We just moved and we've been getting our place fixed up."

"What's the check for?"

"It's for the interview we did in Arcila when I came to the market and we talked."

I thanked him for the check and I asked him why he had moved to Tangier.

He said, "Because I just inherited some money from my family in America, and I'm going to take Driss to London so he can have an operation on his leg."

I said, "That's very nice and generous of you to take Driss to London. His leg would never get fixed here in Morocco."

We stayed there talking for a while. I told them that they should come up to Mr. Miles's house on the Mountain. I told them how beautiful it was there.

Haskell said, "I don't think Miles and I would get along. We seem to have problems."

"Well, you should go and see Ann. You don't live far from her. She misses you."

"Oh, of course. I'm going to see Ann before we leave for London, and we're going to stay there for three weeks."

I said "Allah ihennikoum" and I left. I walked to my house. I wanted to see if my wife needed any money.

I opened the door and my wife wasn't home. My mother-in-law was there all alone.

I said, "What happened? Where is my wife?"

She said, "She went to see her sister."

I asked her if they needed anything. She said, "No." I said, "Allah ihennik."

I walked until I was up by the Spanish Consulate. When I got there, the bus was there. I went down to the market. I did the shopping and took a bus back. Then I started walking up to the house.

When I got there, I took the food to the kitchen.

Mr. Miles asked me: "Did you have a good trip to the city?"

I said, "Yes. I did."

"Listen, Larbi. The summer is almost over. In two weeks I'll be going back to the city."

I stayed working for Mr. Miles today and tomorrow. Two weeks went by. One afternoon Mr. Miles said, "We're leaving tomorrow. Get your things ready by tomorrow afternoon."

I told him I was ready. I didn't have very much to take with me.

The next day we had everything ready. Mr. Miles called a taxi, and we waited until it came. We put our luggage in the taxi, and we drove away. We rode down the hill. That was the last time I was up on the Mountain.

16 / Time Magazine

The taxi drove to Mr. Miles's apartment. I helped with the luggage. He paid me for that last week, and I said "Allah ihennik."

I went home and my wife and the whole family were there.

She said, "Why are you home so early? Aren't you working anymore?"

I said, "No. The job is all over."

"What are you going to do now?"

"I don't know. I might go to Europe."

We had a baby girl, and my wife was six months pregnant. I began to think about what I was going to do. I needed to work much harder than ever before with another baby on the way.

I stayed without work for about three weeks. One day I heard knocking, and there was Mr. Miles.

He said, "I'm glad I found you at home."

"Why? Do you have any good news for me? What is the news you have for me?"

"There's a magazine called Time magazine in America. They want to send a reporter here to talk to you about the book. What do you think? Do you want to talk to him?"

"What is it all about?"

"The reporter wants to ask you questions and talk to you about the book—that's all."

"Ouakha. I'll talk to him."

"Well, he's going to be here next week. How do you want to arrange the meeting?"

"I'll come to your house and talk to him. Or you bring him here."

"I don't know."

"Why don't I prepare lunch for the two of you. And after we have lunch, we'll talk."

We settled on the day. I told Mr. Miles to come with the reporter at 12:00.

That day I went down to the market and shopped. We planned to have pinchitos for lunch. It was a very sad day in my house. My wife and I had been fighting since we got up in the morning. I tried to explain to my wife why I wanted to go to Europe, but she wouldn't understand.

She said, "You can't leave us here."

I said, "I can't count on anyone here to help me. Look how many people I know, how many people there are in my family. When I'm broke, I can't get one franc from anybody."

We made the lunch and we waited. Twelve o'clock came and we waited and waited. One o'clock came. Two o'clock came. Three o'clock came, and no one appeared.

I thought that maybe Mr. Miles and the reporter had had trouble finding my house, but I knew that couldn't be. Mr. Miles knew where I lived.

My wife said, "Let's eat. The food's already cold."

We had our lunch. We washed the dishes and put everything away. About thirty minutes later, I heard a car coming up the street. I went outside and there was Lalla Ann with another woman and a man. I had already made up my mind not to talk to the reporter. When I saw Lalla Ann with them, I changed my mind. She'd gone to the trouble to bring them over. It wouldn't be right not to talk to them.

I asked them what had happened. Nobody said anything. I asked them to come in.

The man said, "I'd like to see where you live."

I showed them the house.

I said, "Why were you late? You were supposed to come at twelve and have lunch. Then we were going to do our interview."

The reporter said, "Why don't you bring your tray and your glasses and your teapot and pretend you're pouring tea, so we can take some pictures."

I brought all those things and I picked up the teapot and pretended to pour. In those pictures he took, I was pouring nothing out of a teapot.

He said, "That's good. That's good. Hold the teapot like that."

"Are you going to use these pictures in the magazine?"

"Yes. That's why I'm taking them."

I began to wonder about the whole thing. It had taken about ten or fifteen minutes.

He said, "Now the interview is over. We're leaving."

I thanked Lalla Ann for bringing the reporter to my house. I shook their hands and said: "Allah ihennikoum." I said to myself, I hope I see some of those pictures.

I said to myself, Don't worry. It doesn't matter. I was never anybody important.

⊕ ⊕ ⊕

Printed March 1985 in Santa Barbara & Ann Arbor
for the Black Sparrow Press by Graham Mackintosh
& Edwards Brothers Inc. Design by Barbara Martin.
This edition is published in paper wrappers;
there are 300 cloth trade copies; 200 hardcover
copies have been numbered & signed by the author;
& 26 lettered copies have been handbound in boards
by Earle Gray & are signed by the author.

I was born in 1937 in a small town called Menarbiyaa. The population is no more than 150 people. The village is 50 miles west of a town called Babtaza.

When I was three years old my mother and my father divorced. My father went down to Fez to teach at the University of Fez. My mother, her new husband, and I moved to Tangier in 1940.

Time went by until 1961 when I met the American novelist, Paul Bowles. I told him that I knew many stories if he was interested in doing a translation from Moghrebi. He said that he was delighted; that I would tell him stories and that he would do the translations. We worked together for one year.

The winter of 1963 Paul Bowles went to America. He met a man named Richard Seaver, an editor at Grove Press, who agreed to publish *A Life Full of Holes.* The book was eventually published in seven languages. I came to America in 1964 and have been here since.